WAMPUS RUMPUS

WAMPUS RUMPUS

A BUBBA THE MONSTER HUNTER NOVELLA

JOHN G. HARTNESS

Charlotte, NC

FALSTAFF
BOOKS

WWW.FALSTAFFBOOKS.COM

Dedicated to Paul Wight - a hell of a rumpus all his own.

S he moved well for somebody with no formal training, keeping her muzzle down unless it was time to shoot something, eyes flicking back and forth over everywhere a threat could materialize, and gliding along in a smooth step that kept her shots tight and her hands steady. A figure swung out from behind the corner of a building, and her MP-7 snapped up, putting a red dot on the man's forehead before moving off to the left as she saw he carried a bag of groceries, not a gun. Then a pair of shapes lunged into view almost simultaneously, one with a shotgun aimed straight at her midsection, and the other with a pistol pressed to the temple of a frightened child. She put two rounds through the face of the man holding the hostage, then swung her barrel over to the other attacker. Just as she brought her gun to bear, all the lights turned red and a loud buzzing sound filled the air.

"Shit!" Geri yelled as the fluorescent lights flickered to life. "There is no way a human being could have taken down both of those guys! Hell, most *monsters* we hunt aren't fast enough to take them out!"

Skeeter's voice, amplified to almost skull-splitting volume and forced through the crappy intercom system strung throughout the building, came from everywhere all at once. Like that movie, only…more annoying. "You're right. The buzzer is to indicate that you're dead, not that you failed. You made the right choice. Sometimes there is no choice that has you walking out of a situation. When that happens, you save everyone you can and go down swinging."

"Well, that's morbid," I muttered.

"But accurate," my fiancée, and our boss, Deputy Director Amy Hall with the Department of Homeland Security's Paranormal Division, replied. "Now are you going to shoot, or you gonna stand there and gripe about how Skeeter runs the *Hogan's Alley* simulation?"

"Little from column A, little from column B," I said as I picked up the mammoth revolver laying on the bench in front of me. I sighted down the eight-inch barrel, laid the front sight across my target, and squeezed off a quick five rounds. Quick for a gun that fires a fifty-caliber, five-hundred-grain round, which isn't really all that quick.

A normal human-sized handgun, you can hold it in one or both hands and squeeze off rounds one right after the other, throwing an absolute hailstorm of projectiles at your target. For a lot of shooters, that's good, because they can't really hit the broad side of a barn and their only chance of hitting something is to send a lot of bullets in its general direction. I was trying out my new sidearm, a Smith & Wesson 500 X-Frame revolver, so there was no world in which I fired that pistol with one hand and then was still able to stay on target. So I squeezed, reset, squeezed, reset, until the five rounds were gone and my ears rang even through the noise-cancelling headphones I wore.

"Not bad," Amy said as I ran the target back to check my accuracy. Three out of five were in the X-ring, which was pretty good. The other two were still good, center mass shots, which would be enough to take down almost anything that I ran into. As long as they could be hurt with bullets, that is. Not everything can. But if bullets would hurt it, this new cannon would kill it. That was pretty much guaranteed. It was slow, though. Revolvers were typically slower than semi-automatics, and the 500 had pretty serious recoil, so it wasn't as fast as Bertha, my old Desert Eagle. But Bertha was gone, and New Gun didn't have a name yet, so that's where we were.

"I think I'm gonna like this thing," I said, turning the pistol over in my hands. It was a pretty weapon, shiny and new, but it still felt a little strange strapping on a gun again after the better part of a year. But our last mission proved to me that not all problems could be solved with charm and diplomacy. Hell, I've never managed to solve *any* problem with charm or diplomacy, but there are also a lot that can't be solved with swords and fists, either. Sometimes you needed to put large holes in bad things. And this beast certainly put large holes in things.

"You done?" Amy asked, drawing her own service weapon. She carries a much more reasonable Glock 19, one of the preferred weapons of law enforcement everywhere. It's neither as ridiculously large nor loud as my pistol, but in Amy's hands is probably even more dangerous. She put ten rounds down range in a matter of seconds, every one landing square in the head ring on her target.

"Yeah, yeah, you're a better shot than me," I grumbled. "But I still bench more than you do." The eternal defense of a man with a bruised ego—upper body strength.

"We could run the obstacle course after this if you like," Amy shot back, one eyebrow climbing in challenge.

"Not a chance. Those psychos put up some new *American Ninja* shit in the gym, and there's no way I'm getting on that.

3

Besides, I deal with all obstacles the same way—by running right through them." We were practicing in half of the CrossFit gym I owned in Atlanta, in a training facility DHS set up for us. The lease from the government helped cover the money the gym lost every month, and gave me a place to shoot where I didn't have to worry about killing a random hunter or other idiot who couldn't respect the "No Trespassing" signs all over my property.

"Okay, gang," Skeeter's voice came back over the intercom, "unless you want to run through the Alley again, it's almost time for the gym to open for the evening crowd, so let's bug out."

I nodded, not that he was looking at me, and started packing up my gear. New Gun went into a pistol case, then that went into a backpack along with all our ammo and Amy's pistol. Geri came over and dropped her spare magazines, safety glasses, and ear protection into the bag with all our gear, then slipped her MP-7 into a duffel bag. When we walked out into the Atlanta sun, we looked like three normal civilians leaving a gym, not super-secret government operatives who had just sent hundreds of rounds of ammunition into steel and paper enemies.

"Taco Mac?" Geri asked as we piled into Amy's Suburban. We'd taken her ride down from my mountain cabin because her Suburban, even heavily armored with bulletproof glass, run-flat tires, and special hidden cargo compartments full of weapons, explosives, and protective gear, *still* got better gas mileage than my F-250. I kept hinting that Homeland should buy me one of the new electric pickups, but Amy kept stubbornly not forgetting that I'd destroyed half a dozen trucks in the last decade. Maybe spending a hundred grand on a vehicle for me wasn't going to make anyone's budget, but I wasn't giving up. If I was known for one thing, it was for being stubborn.

Okay, I was probably known for being carelessly destructive, horrifically smartassed, possibly psychotic, often smelly, usually rude, and potentially completely unhinged, too. But I'm sure stubborn figured into the equation somewhere.

"I could go for wings," I said.

"Nope!" Amy and Geri said in unison.

"I am not spending two-plus hours in this truck with you and your wing farts," Geri said. "I'll shoot you myself."

"I'll buy the ammo," Amy said. "We're going to Fox Brothers, and you're *not* ordering anything extra spicy."

Good. I wanted barbecue anyway. Wings are awesome, one of my favorite food groups. But dudes with facial hair understand that wings are a constant balancing act between sauce in mouth and sauce in beard. I just wasn't up for all the maintenance wings would require, not after a full morning of training. "Can I get banana pudding?" I asked.

"Does banana pudding give you gas?" Geri asked.

"No more than anything else. I'm a dude, and I'm pushing forty. Most everything gives me gas." With that thought looking heavy over our heads, we rolled out toward the best barbecue in the city of Atlanta, and the best banana pudding. Maybe I'd just have pudding for lunch. A *lot* of pudding.

I woke up from my barbecue coma just about the time we turned off the main road to head up the gravel path to my cabin back in the woods outside Dalton, Georgia. It was a good day. The sun was shining, the birds were singing, I had a belly full of good barbecue, and my Bulldogs were back-to-back National Football Champions. What in the world could go wrong?

"Well, shit," I said, looking out the windshield. Skeeter was sitting on my front porch in a nice wooden rocker with his feet up on the railing. He had a Cheerwine in his hand and a white plastic bag by his feet. I could see the telltale shape of a six-pack in the bag, and that was never good.

Skeeter's my best friend. Has been since middle school. We were a little bit of an odd pair in our youth—the big muscular football player and the gay Black nerd who weighed a hundred twenty pounds soaking wet. But it worked for us. I kept Skeeter from getting his ass beat by racist homophobes who didn't like comic books, and he kept me from flunking Trigonometry. We'd gone to college together, gotten jobs with the government together, gotten shipped off to Fairyland together, gotten fired by the government together, and saved the world at least twice.

And I still never liked it when he showed up on my porch unannounced with booze. It meant something was seriously screwed up, and I was probably going to have to punch a lot of people before it was un-screwed. Or maybe I'd just have to punch one person (or monster, cryptid, magical being, or unicorn—I don't discriminate, I just punch), but I'd have to punch them an awful lot. Either way, Skeeter bringing booze as a bribe meant that somebody was in for an ass-whooping. I hoped it wasn't me this time.

I got out of the passenger seat, blinking my eyes against the bright sun, and regretted once again that I'd never developed a taste for sunglasses. I'm a big dude, and I frequently have to leave places in a hurry. Sunglasses are one of those things that end up getting left places, or flying off my head while I run, or getting squished when I jump into my truck and haul ass out of whatever shitstorm I've found myself in. Regardless, I don't usually have shades, and it was really bright.

I held out a hand as I climbed the steps. "Beer me," I said.

Skeeter reached down beside his chair without breaking the rhythm of his rocking and passed me a bottle of Miller

Lite. I twisted the top off and flipped the cap toward a small trash can Amy kept on the porch. Probably just for that purpose, now that I thought about it.

"What's up, Skeet?" I asked. "Can't be too terrible, I reckon."

"Why's that?" Geri asked, clomping up the steps behind me, snagging a beer for herself, and sitting in the rocker by Skeeter.

I held up my bottle. "Domestic beer. If it was really bad, Skeeter woulda sprung for better beer. At least a micro-brew."

"You know I'm not about the hipster beer, Bubba," Skeeter protested.

"You literally have half a dozen craft brew t-shirts in your closet," I reminded him. "And you get beer shipped to you from all over the country. You're the most hipster beer drinker I've ever met. Now what's up?"

"Well, my taste in beer aside, we've got a case," Skeeter said.

"Pretty sure I'm the one who decides if we've got a case or not," Amy said, leaning on the rail beside me. "That whole 'Deputy Director' thing, you know."

"Yeah, but this one's right in our wheelhouse. It's in Tennessee, it's a monster, and there's almost no chance that it involves demons, Nazis, fairies, dragons, or CrossFit werewolves."

"I'm interested," I said, draining my beer and reaching for another. Shut up. I drink fast, but hydration is important, and it was domestic light beer, anyway.

"Then strap in, Bubba, because we're going after a wampus cat!" Skeeter and I high-fived at the idea of chasing down one of my bucket list cryptids after all these years.

Geri, however, was unimpressed. "Um, guys," she said, holding up a hand. "What the hell is a wampus cat?"

2

F ive minutes later, we were in my living room and Skeeter had made a laptop materialize from some- where. Hell, for all I knew, it might have been living under my couch cushions, just waiting for the day when Skeeter needed to hijack my television and give a video presentation on the magical, mythical, wampus cat.

The wampus cat ranges from hilarious to horrifying, depending on the version of its origin and who's telling the story. Some Native tribes have the creature as a woman condemned to wear that shape after hiding under the pelt of a mountain lion to observe a sacred ritual. Other tales have it as a natural creature with a large, spiked ball on its tail, while some say that the creature can teleport, popping into existence, taking a swipe at any idiot who came to close to its lair, and poofing away again. I had never paid too much attention to origin stories, but it was one of the few cryptids native to the South- eastern U.S. that I hadn't been sent out hunting at some point.

Now a fair number of the things I have been assigned to chase turned out to be something else entirely, like the chupacabra attacks that were really vampires who ate cows and not people, or the vampire ballerinas, or the troll under the bridge in South Carolina. No wait, that one was pretty much exactly as advertised. Big, ugly, mean as hell, lived under a bridge…yep, it was a troll, all right. Until it was troll parts scattered all over Falls Park in downtown Greenville. I even felt a little bad about the mess from that one. Not bad enough to help clean it up, but there was a touch of regret there.

But now Skeeter had some doohickey connected to my TV and was beaming drawings, fuzzy vacation photos with weird shapes in the background, and a skipping, out of focus video that made the famous Bigfoot video of the dude in a monkey suit look like Scorsese.

"The wampus cat is generally considered harmless, unless its home is threatened. Or its children. If you come upon a wampus cat with young, you really want to be somewhere else, and quickly. The creature has powerful jaws, razor-sharp claws, and is a hell of an ambush predator, so don't forget to look up."

"What about the spiky ball on its tail? Is that a weapon, too?" I asked.

Skeeter nodded. "Yes. If it's real. It shows up in some legends and not in others, so I'm not sure if the stories are accurate, if they got the wampus cat confused with something like a gowrow, or if there's a random ankylosaurus running around the wilds of North America."

"So no one has ever captured one of these things?" Geri asked.

"Not that we know of," Skeeter replied.

Amy nodded. "There are records of three different Hunters being sent to capture, rehome, or destroy a wampus cat, but they all reported being unable to locate the creature.

The last time anyone was dispatched on a wampus cat call was 1984."

"So our tech is way better," Skeeter said.

"And we're less likely to be actively on coke while we're hunting," I added.

Amy shot me a dark look, but I just shrugged. My grandfather was hunting back in those days, as was my dad. Pop was pretty straight-laced back then, but by all reports, my grandfather would definitely be on the list of Hunters likely to be found snorting lines off a stripper's butt in the bathroom of a topless club when he was supposed to be chasing monsters.

"Wait, hunting while high is an option?" Geri asked.

"Not for you," I said. "I'm in your line of fire way too often for me to be down with you imbibing anything that might give you the shakes."

Geri shrugged. "Not an unreasonable concern, I guess. What else do we need to know, Skeeter?"

"Well, this sighting was reported in the mountains around Pigeon Forge, so it won't be too bad a trip to get there," Skeeter said, but something in his expression told me there was more coming, and I wasn't going to like it.

"What else?" I asked, putting a little bit of threat in my tone. It would probably carry more weight if Skeeter didn't know full well I'd never actually beat his ass, but I hoped maybe he'd forget that fact for a second or two and be intimidated enough to tell me what I needed to know.

Not so much. He just looked me in the eye and said, "You ain't gonna like it, but I don't want to hear any bitching. You need the money."

"What money?" I asked. "We're doing alright. The gym pays for itself, freelancing for Homeland covers most of the bills, and if I run short on cash, I just call on my sugar mama." I gave Amy what I thought was a saucy grin, but the flat stare she sent back in my direction told me that she somehow didn't find me as hilarious as I do. That always confuses me. I think I'm amazing, but I guess my sense of humor is just ahead of my time. Like Oscar Wilde, or Gallagher. Misunderstood geniuses, both of them.

"You still have a roof over your head only because you don't have a mortgage," Skeeter said. "Homeland has been decent, but that new pistol uses expansive ammo, and I bet the first time you turn in for reimbursement of that, you're going to get a strongly worded memo about the virtues of the nine-millimeter round."

"I bet anyone who thinks a nine mil is a reasonable sized bullet has never stood toe to butt-nekkid toe with a grumpy Sasquatch," I said. "Because that wouldn't even push through the body hair on one of those beasties, much less their thick hide."

"You know that, and I know that, but I'm pretty sure the DHS accountants don't know that," Skeeter said. "Which is why I wanted to introduce you to our newest employer—"

"Oh, what the absolute hell is this?!?" I asked, coming up out of my chair at the sight of the man walking in my front door. "I did *not* agree to this shit."

"Good to meet you, too, Mr. Brabham. My name is Father Matthew Ortega, and I am your new liaison with the Church. I'm happy to say that after some...shakeup within its structure over the past few years, that you have been reinstated as the official Southeastern Regional Monster Hunter for the Holy Roman Catholic Church. If you want the job, of course."

I gave this new guy a long look up and down. He wasn't very big. Not much bigger than Skeeter, really. So I'd put him at five ten, and skinny, maybe a hundred fifty pounds soaking wet. He was youngish, maybe thirty, with a neatly trimmed dark goatee showing not the slightest hint of gray, and close-cropped dark brown hair cut in a professional style. Now contrast that with my shaggy brown locks hanging down around my ears, courtesy of an impromptu haircut from a bunch of assholes in North Carolina, Skeeter's gleaming black pate, and Geri's purple and pink-streaked black hair. Amy kept her blond hair neatly cut a little longer than her shoulders, the only one among us who looked like she could actually go work in an office. Good thing she was the only one of us who ever had to go work in an office, then. But this dude? Take his collar and cassock off and he could fit right in at an insurance agency or a call center. He just looked…normal.

"You know who we are?" I asked.

"I do," Father Matthew replied.

"You know what we do?"

"I do."

"You know how to say anything else, or are we gonna end up married after another 'I do'?" I asked.

"You're not my type," he said. "Too much body hair and I'm not into tattoos."

"Or dudes," I added.

"I didn't say that," the priest replied.

"I thought you still couldn't be gay and be a Catholic priest?" Geri piped up.

"I'm Episcopalian."

"But you're our liaison with the Catholic Church?" I asked.

"It's a little complicated, but just like you aren't required to be Catholic to hunt for the Church, I don't have to be Catholic to liaise with them for you. The position doesn't actually require a priest of any denomination, but the Church leadership felt that someone with an official title might be more effective in helping you—"

"They thought if I saw the collar, I'd be less likely to beat the shit out of you and throw you out into the dirt," I said, cutting him off with a wave of my hand.

"Yeah, that. Now since I don't want to have my ass kicked, and this cassock looks better without me being thrown in the dirt, do you want the gig or should I just piss off?"

As much as I wanted to tell him to kiss every inch of my massive furry ass, I looked at my friends and could tell they really wanted me to at least hear this dude out. "Okay, how much are you paying? Because I'm gonna need a hell of a raise after the way the Church tossed me to the curb when they found out I'm part fairy. Racist pricks."

He quoted a number, and it wasn't just larger than my last salary with the Church, it was *way* larger. Now he had my attention. "Well, Padre, why don't you have a seat. You want a beer? Wine? Do we have any wine?"

"Yes, we have wine," Amy said.

"No, thank you," Father Matthew said. "But now that I have your attention, let's look at the information we have on this supposed wampus cat."

F ather Matthew came prepared. He handed Skeeter a thumb drive, and in seconds we were looking at satellite pictures of the woods around Pigeon Forge. He zoomed in, and I thought for a second I could tell where Dollywood was, but he scrolled sideways before I could see any cool roller coasters.

"Where did these pictures come from?" I asked. "Is this one of those super-secret Catholic satellites I've heard about?"

Father Matthew sighed. "Secret Catholic Satellites? Is that like Jewish Space Lasers?"

"I don't know," I replied. "Jewish folk ain't exactly what you'd call thick on the ground in North Georgia, so I ain't had the chance to ask anybody who might actually know. There's that woman up in Cleveland. She might have more info."

"Well, regardless, these images didn't come from a secret Catholic spy satellite. See the little multi-colored circle in the bottom corner? This is Google Maps."

"Oh." Everything about this presentation just got a lot less interesting. I got up and headed for the kitchen to grab another beer, thought about it for a second, and just grabbed the whole six-pack. I didn't know how many PowerPoint slides I was going to have to sit through, but I wasn't doing that shit sober.

"As you can see," Father Matthew continued, just as though I hadn't wandered off in the middle of his dog and pony show. "There are hundreds of acres of heavily wooded mountainous terrain in the Pigeon Forge area, giving the wampus cat, if that is in fact what we're looking for, plenty of places to hide."

He tapped his phone, and a string of red dots appeared on the map. Another tap, and a series of yellow dots popped up. "These are confirmed and potential sightings that have been reported in the region within the last eighteen months."

I leaned forward to get a better look. "Yellow are the maybes and red are the definite sightings?" I asked.

"As definite as cryptid sightings get, yes."

"Looks like they're running east from something." I pointed at the TV, and Father Matthew passed me a laser pointer. I mean, I don't know what kind of bag of holding he had sewn into the pockets of his robe, but who the hell runs around with a laser pointer in their pocket? Unless you're a middle manager or a cat person, why do you even own one of those things?

Regardless, I took the pointer from the priest and aimed it at the screen. "See how the yellow dots make an arc behind the red ones? I'm gonna guess that all those sightings took place far from any town or even a trailer park. Probably way back in the woods somewhere, and the critter was spotted by a hunter or a fisherman. Or maybe teenagers looking for a place to hook up or get loaded."

"Yes, the unconfirmed sightings are older than the red dots," Matthew confirmed.

"So these red dots are in more populated areas, and the people who saw the wampus are less likely to be stoned out of their gourd or straight up crazy," I said.

"I probably would have used different words, but basically correct," Father Matthew said. I thought there might have been a hint of a smile, but just a hint. This dude was wound pretty tight.

"Okay, so is there a plan in that slideshow of yours?" I asked. Geri and Amy were just sitting on the couch watching while I tried to see if I could push the skinny priest off his game.

"Not really," he admitted with a hint of red creeping into his cheeks. "I've never done any kind of field work. Honestly, I'm pretty new to the job. I understand that my predecessor left some big shoes to fill, and it's taken the Church a while to find the proper replacement for this region."

"You ain't replacing nobody," I said. "Uncle Father Joe was family, and even if you turn out to be the best monster hunter liaison in the world, you ain't gonna be family. Besides, I thought the Church already had a dude taking care of my territory. That Dallas Hunter dude or whatever his name is."

"Hunter Houston," Father Matthew said with a slight grimace. "He's good at what he does, but…well, you're better. You have more experience, more successful resolutions, and a strong team built in. We will likely continue to utilize Mr. Houston from time to time, but the Church feels that it's time to…"

"Get the starters off the bench," I said.

"Get their heads out of their asses and re-hire the pros," Geri added.

"Call in the big guns," Skeeter finished.

Father Matthew nodded. "Yes, all of those things. There are monsters out there in the world, Bubba. Someone has to hunt them down and keep the world safe for humanity. You're that someone."

Well, shit. I was going to do it. I was going to take the Church's money, and hunt the Church's monsters, choke down my dislike for organized religion, and forgive them for firing my ass. Because he was right. This was what I was put here to do. I hunt monsters. And I did need the money, apparently.

"Okay."

I heard Skeeter let out a massive sigh of relief, with a slightly smaller one coming from Amy. Geri just clapped her hands, jumped up from the couch, and sprinted to her room. I assumed she was going to spend some quality time with her favorite gun. Or her favorite knife. Or maybe her favorite high explosive ordinance.

Father Matthew gave me a relieved smile. "Good. I'm very glad to hear that. I have rooms booked for us at a hotel right outside Pigeon Forge. They're expecting us tonight."

"Pretty sure of yourself, aren't you?" I asked.

"No," Skeeter said. "He was sure of me. You need this, Bubba. And if Father Matt couldn't get you to see that, I was going to bully you into doing it. Now get packed. Pigeon Forge is only a couple hours from here, but y'all all gonna need showers before you spend three hours in a car together. Every one of you smells like gunpowder and sweat."

"Two of my favorite perfumes," I said, raising an eyebrow at Amy.

"Gonna have to put a pin in that one, loverboy," she said. "We're on a schedule, and this time it's not mine. But I'm calling dibs on the shower now that I'm the one with the longest hair." She gave me a saucy grin and hopped off the couch, heading for the back of the house.

I ran my fingers through my hair, shorter than it had been since I blew out my knee playing college football. "That's just mean," I said, but I doubted Amy could hear me over her own laughter.

WE GOT TO THE HOTEL, a Fairfield Inn just off I-40, and I raised an eyebrow at Father Matt when he came back to where we waited for him to handle everything and handed a key to Amy, then turned around and started walking toward an elevator.

"Where's Geri sleeping, Padre?" I asked. "Because vow of celibacy or no, I don't think she's gonna dig crashing with you."

Father Matthew stopped and turned around, looking at me in confusion. "I got one room for the men, and another room for the ladies. That seemed to be the most logical and economical course of action."

I laughed out loud in the middle of the hotel lobby. "Dude, I ain't bunking with you when my fiancée is sleeping in the same building. Amy and I room together."

"And as much as it hurts to let these words pass my lips, Bubba's right," Geri said. "I'm not sharing a room with you, Father. No offense, but I know more about Episcopalians than Bubba does. You guys don't take vows of celibacy, do you?"

Father Matthew blushed a little. I reckon there ain't too many days of the week he ends up chatting about his sex life in a public place. "No, we do not."

"Are you gay?" Geri asked.

"I don't know that my sexuality is any of your business," the priest replied.

"Yeah, it wouldn't be most days," Geri replied. "But if you're not into girls, I'd be more likely to share a room with you. Like two percent more likely, because no matter who you're into, I just met you like six hours ago, and I am not all that interested in rooming with a complete stranger."

Father Matthew stammered around for a minute, looking back and forth between Geri and me, then turned to Amy for help. She shook her head and held up both hands in surrender. "Not my circus, not my monkeys, Padre. This is a Church job, so you're dealing with the accommodations. If I plop my DHS credit card down on the counter of an unapproved hotel and it's not a matter of life or apocalypse, I'll be filling out forms in triplicate until Bubba's hair grows back."

"Still mean," I said.

She blew me a kiss. "Babe, we've been together for close to ten years now and these past few weeks is the first time since we've been together that the back of your neck hasn't been covered by long hair. You've always claimed to be a redneck, but it's been really funny to see your neck actually turn red in the sun. *And* when you get embarrassed, usually about not having any hair. So yeah, I'm going to give you shit until your hair grows back."

"It's a good thing I love you," I grumbled.

"Damn right," Amy said, and hopped up on tiptoes to give me a quick peck on the lips. I was a little surprised. We aren't much for public displays of affection, normally, but I was happy to take it.

"Heh," came a voice from across the lobby. "She's got you whipped, boy." I looked over to where a trio of middle-aged rednecks sat in the small "lounge" area, clustered around the remnants of a twelve-pack of Bud, with two more cases sitting on the carpet next to the small table they sat around.

I opened my mouth to reply, but Amy squeezed my arm in that unmistakable "please don't start a fight and destroy the hotel because we'll have to find another place to sleep and I'd very much appreciate it if you would not allow your baser Neanderthal instincts to dictate your actions for the next thirty seconds." Yes, that's a lot to pack into one squeeze of a forearm, but Amy could be very eloquent when she wanted to be.

And I, with the glorious stubbornness of all middle-aged rednecks, even those of us whose necks haven't seen the sun for the better part of twenty years, ignored her completely. "Well, boss," I said, giving the redneck who spoke my best "eat shit and die" grin. "If you had a woman like this, you'd do anything she asked for, too."

And of course that was the opening Tweedles Dumb, Dumber, and Dumbest were hoping for. They all hopped up from the table and stomped over to me, chests puffed out and mock fury all over their faces. "You calling my wife ugly, asshole?" asked Tweedledumber, the lead redneck who first called out to me.

"Nah," I said. "I wouldn't insult a woman, especially not one who ain't here to defend herself." I felt Amy relax a little beside me, like she was relieved I'd finally matured enough not to start a fight with every single idiot that stepped up to me.

And here I thought she knew me. "You, on the other hand…well, you're standing right here, so I can call you a fat, inbred, gap-toothed dipshit with nothing better to do than sit around in a half-drunk circle jerk with your two boyfriends here looking for entertainment in the lobby of a Tennessee Fairfield Inn. See? I don't have to call your wife ugly. I can just imply by everything I say about your dumb ass that she's either so butt-ugly she could only get a husband that no other woman would look at, or blind. Or ugly *and* blind, that's also an option. Hell, maybe she's blind, ugly, and stupid, because if she married you, there's gotta be some first cousins married not too many branches up in her family tree."

I could almost feel Amy shaking her head beside me as I

played Antagonize the Morons. I would have felt bad, but I needed some therapy right then. I'd been trapped in a vehicle for three hours with a brand-new priest, who made my whole truck smell like incense and fresh soap, completely overriding the carefully cultivated aroma of Chili Cheese Fritos and Cheerwine that I had built up over months of eating on the road. I needed to punch something, and I was afraid if I didn't beat the shit out of these idiots, I'd do something stupid, like running around in the woods at night looking for a wampus cat.

Yeah, I know running around the woods at night looking for monsters is literally my job, but as far as excuses to get in a friendly little scrap go, that one was pretty good. Either way, it worked. It took Tweedledumber almost ten seconds to sort through everything I said and decide that yep, I did in fact insult him, his wife, and the last few generations of his wife's family.

Then he punched me in the face and the fun really started.

4

I staggered back, neither surprised nor really all that off-balance from his punch, but I wanted it to show very clearly on the security footage that I didn't throw the first punch. That has been important in many conversations throughout my life, all of them involving myself and one or more members of law enforcement. And I was pretty sure we were gonna be introduced to the local constabulary before long.

But like Ke$ha, I was ready to go "until the po-po shut us down." Shut up. I like Ke$ha. How could you not like someone with honest hips? So once I was sure the cameras had recorded the start of the fight, I figured I should try to end it as fast as possible. Not because I was afraid of these idiots hurting one of us, or earning significant jail time, but mostly because I didn't want to give Geri time to really get going. To say she's a little…"bloodthirsty" would be putting it mildly. If one of these idiots got a lucky punch in and actually managed to hurt her, they'd be picking viscera out of the ceiling lights in this lobby for *weeks*.

So I reeled back way more than I needed to, put a hand

on the registration desk, and pushed off, tackling Tweedle-dumbest and taking him to the ground, where I started punching him. Not much, just enough to get his attention. I have to be more careful about hitting humans since I got back from Fairyland a couple years ago. Seems like being exposed to a realm of pure magic jump-started the fairy magic in me, and now I heal better, hit harder, and…well, I probably run a little faster, but I try not to run at all if possible. So I hit harder and heal faster. And since I didn't want to turn this guy's skull into a jigsaw puzzle, I held back with my punches.

Of course, Geri jumped right in and went after Twee-dledumb like a spider monkey on crystal meth. She leapt up on the dude, wrapped her legs around his waist, and started punching him in the face while he spun around in circles trying to dislodge the psychotic starfish that was wrapped around his face pounding his nose into hamburger.

What surprised me was that it was Father Matthew who leapt into the fray next, while Amy just stood by the front desk recording everything on her phone. The little priest didn't hesitate; he just stepped right up to Tweedledumber and punched him in the nose. No muss, no fuss, just a straight left jab to the face. Tweedledumber looked flum-moxed at being attacked by a slim, middle-aged man wearing a priest's collar. It had to feel like getting mugged by Father Mulcahy.

I turned my attention back to Tweedledumbest when he managed to buck me off and scramble to his feet. I rolled over and pulled myself up using one of the lobby couches, then almost fell over that same couch when he caught me with a massive right hook that made me wonder for a second if I was the only person in the room that wasn't completely human. Dude was *stout*. Then I decided that it had just been too long since I got in a real, fair fight, so I put my guard up and grinned at him.

"Let's dance, dickweed," I said, spitting out a glob of blood onto the lobby floor. We were one hundred percent not gonna be allowed to stay in this hotel, or maybe any hotel in the chain, ever again.

Tweedledumbest came at me with his hands up, bobbing and weaving like he'd watched *Creed* too many times. I like those movies, but they don't teach anybody how to box, much less how to fight in the lobby of a Tennessee hotel. While he ducked from side to side and jabbed the air, I took two steps forward, wrapped my arms around him, pinning his arms to his ribcage, and gave him a belly-to-belly duplex into a coffee table. Glass flew everywhere, wood splintered, and Tweedledumbest let out a yell like a cow woken from a deep slumber by a group of drunk high school football players pushing it over onto its side.

Pro tip—if you're going to do this, make sure you don't tip the only bull in the pasture. They don't take it well.

Tweedledumbest didn't take it well either, writhing in pain on the lobby floor calling me all kinds of names, some of them even accurate. I'll own "fat redneck piece of crap" and "giant dipshit" because those are pretty accurate a lot of the time. But all the stuff he was yelling about my mother? Nah, that's not cool, man.

It was not cool enough that I stomped on his nuts to shut him up. I know, it's not really sporting. But that's the differ-ence between boxing, whether you learned it from Michael B. Jordan movies or from someone who could actually teach you to throw a punch—rules. In boxing or MMA there are all these rules about where you can hit somebody. In a real fight, where the other person, or creature in my case, is trying to you permanently damage or flat-out kill you, there are no rules. You need to kick some dumbass in the balls to keep him from breaking your neck? Kick away. You need to bite some dipshit's ear off so he'll stop choking you? Chomp to your heart's content.

Tweedledumbest was one of those rednecks who has spent his whole life being the baddest dude in the room, and being backed up by the second and third toughest guys in the room. When he ran into somebody who was bigger and badder than him, with friends who didn't give a shit how tough his buddies were, he didn't know how to adapt. Me and mine are used to fighting monsters that would rather rip our guts out and wear them as necklaces than chitchat, so three dumbasses in a hotel lobby were not much of a challenge. That said, the longer any fight goes on, the more likely someone I like is going to get hurt, so it was in our best interests to get everything settled quickly. And stomping on a dude's nutsack settles stuff pretty damned quick.

I looked over to Geri, and she was still riding Tweedledumb like some kind of weird new Dollywood ride, with one arm around his throat and the other one slamming into the side of his head in quick little punches. Father Matthew was dismantling Tweedledumber piece by piece with kicks, punches, and throws. When he saw me stop moving out of the corner of his eye, he stopped playing around, took a step back, and kicked the dude right on the point of his chin.

Tweedledumber was a good six-three, giving him better than six inches on Father Matty, but the skinny priest just stood flat-footed and kicked him in the face. Tweedledumber fell backward and stretched out his full length along the carpet, unconscious before he hit the ground. Father Matthew turned back to me and gave me a little nod, as if to say, "Okay, my shit is handled."

Geri was a little more direct in her finish, but no less impressive. One second she was wrapped around Tweedledumb's torso like moss on an oak tree, and the next she vaulted off his shoulders, flipped over the dude's head, spun around, and leveled a pistol at Tweedledumb's face. I have no idea where she drew the gun from, and am not nearly stupid enough to ask. She reached into a back pocket, pulled out her credentials, and yelled out, "Homeland Security, nobody fucking move!"

And that's when the cops showed up.

And by "showed up" I mean it seemed like every cop within fifty miles must have rolled up into the Fairfield Inn parking lot with their sirens blaring and lights flashing and basically guaranteeing that nobody in the hotel was getting anything like a late-afternoon nap. No fewer than six cop cars of various vintage—sheriff, police, highway patrol— slewed into the lot fishtailing and threatening to trash any vehicle in their way.

"Anybody scratches my truck and I'm gonna have to go back to jail," I yelled to Geri.

"I am *not* bailing your ass out of a Tennessee jail, Bubba!" Geri replied, then thumped Tweedledumb right between the eyes with the butt of her Glock. He didn't slump to the floor immediately unconscious like he would have in a Jason Statham movie, but he did fall to his knees and clutch his bleeding forehead with both hands, removing him from the fight just as effectively.

I lost count of how many cops poured through the front doors of the hotel after eight, but they didn't stop coming for a while past that. All I could really keep track of was the number of guns pointed directly at me, and that number topped out at five—two shotguns and three sidearms from a mix of different uniforms and one fat man in a sport coat with a badge hanging around his neck. I put my hands up over my head and waited for Geri to sort shit out.

Yeah, I know, technically I was probably the senior member of the team, and either Amy or me should have been the one to step up and smooth things over with the local constabulary. But there are a couple of problems with that. First, while I have a Department of Homeland Security badge, it's not worth the tin it's stamped out of. I don't actually work for DHS; I'm a contractor. I don't have any authority to deal with state or local law enforcement. I go out in the woods hunting monsters, and Uncle Sam sends me a check. Interfacing with overblown rednecks who peaked in tenth grade is a job for people who actually get health insurance.

The other problem is my general disdain for most local cops. I'm not saying that the training is substandard or that a lot of the guys working as small-town cops are in it for some kind of twisted power trip, but I might have said that very thing a couple hundred times, usually when I was in the process of telling a small-town cop to kiss my ass. Which was usually quickly followed by me getting arrested. All the charges were always dropped, but I still don't have the best history with defusing situations, so I decided that we might actually be better off with the heavily armed psychopath dealing with the authority figures than with me in that role.

And Geri dealt with them just fine. After Tweedledumb collapsed to the floor clutching his busted gourd, Geri just swung her pistol over to the first cop in line. "Stop right there or I'll put a bullet in your skull!"

That announcement had two immediate reactions. One, every gun that had been aimed at me was now pointed right at Geri. Two, everybody in the lobby froze in place. It was like they were in that really bad Batman movie and Arnold Schwarzenegger had just iced them over.

I stepped a little out of the line of fire and folded my arms over my chest. She obviously had a plan, and I couldn't wait to see what it was.

ood," Geri said, raising the barrel of her pistol so it no longer pointed straight at a cop's face. "Now that I've got your attention, let's all holster our weapons and talk this out like grownups."

"How about you put your gun on the ground and we won't shoot you?" asked a young cop standing right next to me. He had his weapon leveled at Geri, but I could see from where I was standing that the safety on his M&P 22 was on. I reached over to my right, snatched the pistol out of his hand, ejected the magazine, and slid the gun and clip into separate back pockets. Then I turned to the rookie, who was staring at me with wide eyes, and punched him in the nose.

I turned back to Geri. "Pardon the interruption," I said. "Please proceed."

Now we were surrounded by a room full of absolutely confused cops. At one point of the triangle, they had a pretty young woman with multicolored hair holding up a badge and yelling about being a federal agent. At another point was a giant redneck who just decked one of their buddies. And the third point of the triangle was occupied by some kind of weird hybrid ninja priest, complete with white collar. Yeah, we were not what they were used to.

All the cops put their guns away, and Geri did the same. Father Matthew and I weren't armed, but from what I'd just seen, the little priest kinda *was* a weapon, so maybe he didn't need one. The Tweedle triplets (Dumb, Dumber, and Dumbest) were all still kinda rolling around on the lobby floor like…well, like they'd just had the shit kicked out of them by a bunch of out-of-towners. Which was pretty much exactly what had happened.

"I am Agent Geraldine Stimson with the Department of Homeland Security. We are in the area investigating a threat to national security. These men assaulted my contractor, and we defended ourselves. Now you can either accept this explanation at face value, drive these idiots to the nearest drunk tank where they spend the next twelve to eighteen hours drying out, or you can try to arrest all of us and have the entire weight of the federal government come down on your shoulders. Trust me, you do not want to feel that weight, gentlemen."

I'd never seen Geri put on her "Official Government Agent" routine, and it was pretty impressive. Judging by the low whistle coming through my earpiece, Skeeter was impressed, too.

"You seeing this, bud?" I whispered, trying to move my mouth as little as possible. I probably either looked like a cow chewing its cud, or like a constipated ventriloquist.

Skeeter understood me, though, and said, "Yeah, I see it. I hacked the hotel's security system and am watching you on the lobby cameras. You really don't have a good side, do you?"

"Not as far as a camera's ever found," I replied. "You hacked the hotel? Can you get our rooms comped?"

"One, I might be stretching things to call what I did hacking. The password is PigeonForgeFairfield, all one word, with the first letter of each word capitalized. Not exactly triple-factor authentication. Two, I could get your room comped, but that would screw the small business that owns the hotel, and thus be a dick move. And three, why do you care what your room costs? The government is paying."

"No, the government wants me to turn in receipts for reimbursement, since I'm a contractor. Geri's room is on Uncle Sam's credit card, and Father Matt's got the Vatican black Amex or whatever, but I'm stuck paying out of pocket and hoping I don't lose the paperwork before I file my expense report."

"A monster hunter doing expense reports." I could hear the little shithead giggling over my earpiece. "What is this world coming to? Fine, your room is comped. But I doubled the rate on Geri's room to compensate."

"Whatever," I replied, turning my attention back to Geri and the po-po. Which would be a really fun name for a bubblegum pop band.

They seemed to have sorted out all their issues, because the cops had the Tweedles in cuffs and the first one was headed for the door. Geri shook hands with a pudgy cop rocking a serious GCM (Generic Cop Mustache), then went over to the terrified desk clerk, who had stood frozen behind the counter throughout the entire fight. I watched as she leaned over the counter, patted the stricken clerk's shoulder, then handed him a flask from her back pocket. The terrified dude took a swig, grimaced, then took another, much longer, pull. He handed the flask back to Geri, who slid it back into her hip pocket and patted him on the cheek, literally the most compassionate move I'd ever seen from her.

She walked over to where I was standing and motioned Father Matthew over as well. "I've got things settled with the cops and the hotel. The cops are going to hold these idiots for a couple days on a drunk and disorderly, which will hopefully give us time to find whatever is running around the woods out there before they get sprung and come looking for us. The desk clerk is going to split the damages between my credit card and yours, Father. It only seemed fair that the Church and the government pay for the mess."

"Can we do that?" I asked. "Separation of church and state and all that?"

Geri gave me a withering glare, and for once I just shut up instead of continuing to poke the bear. If this bear was going to pick up the tab for the wrecked coffee table, busted chairs, and ripped couch that we left strewn around the lobby, I should probably keep my big mouth shut for once.

"In exchange," Geri continued, "we will do our best not to do anything else while we're here that gets the police called to our location, and if we do decide to do anything that requires law enforcement's attention, we promise not to do it here in the hotel. Those are the conditions on which I kept us out of jail and in the hotel. Nod your head if you understand me, Bubba."

I nodded, then held up my left hand, middle finger extended, to the nearest security camera as Skeeter's laughter almost deafened me. "Got it. Don't start any fights where the cops get called, and if I do get the cops called on me, do it away from the hotel. I think I can manage that."

"Good plan," Geri replied. "Because if you get us thrown out of this hotel, we're either sleeping in the truck or driving a long-ass way to find someplace else to crash, because the front desk guy swears that if there's any more trouble out of us that he'll get us blacklisted from every hotel within a hundred miles."

"I'm probably already banned from half of them," I said. "I can't stay in a Holiday Inn or Sheraton anywhere east of the

Mississippi anymore. Not since the unfortunate incident with the selkie in the bathtub that one time in Birmingham."

"I don't even want to know," Geri said. "Now can we please go to our rooms, get a shower, and find someplace to eat? I worked up an appetite kicking that guy's ass."

———

AN HOUR later and we were sitting at a Cracker Barrel two exits away from the hotel. There was a Ruby Tuesday across the hotel parking lot, but they serve booze, and their proximity to the Fairfield was not a plus in this situation, because the likelihood of me punching somebody and/or breaking furniture increases dramatically with the application of alcohol, and I wanted to put distance between me and the hotel before I entered any potentially fraught situations. Like dinner.

So I had a plate piled high with chicken and dumplings, fried okra, French fries, and one lonely little broccoli tree breaking up the taupe landscape of my dinner plate. Amy ordered a hamburger steak with mashed potatoes, gravy, onions, and asparagus, referring to the thermonuclear fart fuel she had on her plate as "self defense" when I raised an eyebrow at her. Geri had a hunk of country-fried steak slathered in gravy with mashed potatoes, more gravy, and a heaping bowl of apple sauce on the side. Father Matthew actually had multiple colors on his plate, since he picked the veggie plate and somehow managed to find three vegetables on the menu that weren't breaded and fried. I was starting to think our new liaison might be a Communist, ordering steamed veggies and unsweetened iced tea in the South. Obviously we were going to have to educate this ol' boy.

"Okay, so our arrival in Tennessee was a little more… eventful than we might have expected, but now that the sun's going down, what do we know about where this wampus might be causing its ruckus?" I asked.

"You're going to make every really awful rhyme with wampus that you can, aren't you?" Geri asked.

"No question," Skeeter replied. We had him conferenced into our meal on Geri's tablet, which we had propped up with a basket of cathead biscuits and a ketchup bottle. "Bubba has never found a joke he wouldn't beat into the ground."

"Well, how do you know a horse is dead if you ain't beat the shit out of its corpse?" I asked.

"Anyway," Geri said around a mouthful of steak-like meat, "all the reports we have of wampus cat sightings are located around water, mostly the Little Pigeon River, with a few mentions north of here around the French Broad River."

"That makes sense," I said. "Wampus cats love water. They swim like otters, and legend says they can stay underwater long enough to drag a man down, hold him beneath the surface until he drowns, then haul the body to shore to eat it."

"How the hell is something the size of a bobcat gonna lug a full-grown human being, waterlogged no less, anywhere, much less up onto the banks of a river?" Skeeter asked.

"Because wampus cats ain't bobcat-sized, Skeet," I replied. "They're big as mountain lions, with an extra set of legs in the middle."

"And tentacles growing out of their backs?" Skeeter shot back. We were starting to get strange looks from neighboring tables for talking to an iPad at the dinner table, but if they couldn't get with the times, that was a "them" problem, and not an "us" problem. "Bubba, you're thinking about a displacer beast."

"What the hell is a displacer beast?" I asked.

"It's a monster from *Dungeons & Dragons*, you big idiot.

Now we ain't chasing stuff out of *Volo's Guide to Monsters*, we're hunting down real-life cryptids, so let's keep everybody else's intellectual property out of our jobs, how about it?" Skeeter raised an eyebrow at me, and I nodded. Now that he mentioned it, I did remember displacer beasts. Skeeter got me hooked on *D&D* video games way after our freshman year of college, and I guess some of the ideas stuck in my head through the weed haze we were wrapped in most of that summer.

"Okay, so a wampus cat is smaller than I thought," I said. "Doesn't change the fact that they love water, so around the French Broad is where we need to be hunting."

"Why not the Little Pigeon River?" Father Matthew asked. "It's a lot closer."

"Yeah, but it runs right through Pigeon Forge and alongside decent-sized highways for a lot of its course," I said. "If the wampus cat has a nest, or lair, or whatever, it won't be near where a bunch of people live. The French Broad runs right by a big patch of undeveloped woods not far from here. If the critter's been seen along both the French Broad and Little Pigeon, it stands to reason the nest is somewhere near both rivers, and they meet up not far from this wooded area."

"I've got something else that backs up Bubba's theory," Skeeter said.

"Yeah?" Geri asked. I don't know when we elected the youngest and least mentally stable member of our team Amy's second-in-command, but the more she took on the role, the further away Geri was from wanting to murder me, which was her whole raison d'etre when we first met. So if it meant I didn't have to lock her bedroom door from the outside anymore, she could be Assistant Boss or whatever. I didn't mind. I mean, it's not like I ever listened to what anybody told me to do anyway, so I could ignore her just as well as I ignore anybody else.

"Yeah," Skeeter continued. "There's a new campground being constructed in that chunk of wilderness bounded by the French Broad and Little Pigeon Rivers. It's possible if the wampus lived in those woods, that its habitat was disturbed by construction, and that accounts for the uptick in sightings."

"Okay, then," I said. "We'll gear up and spend a night tromping around in the woods. Again."

"Yippee," Geri said.

"Look on the bright side," I said. "It ain't a swamp this time."

She shot me the bird as I flagged down our waitress, a matronly woman with a lavender rinse in her hair and a scandalized expression at the profane gesture she saw Geri make. I ordered three peach cobblers to make sure we had enough energy for a long night of wampus hunting. Then I got dessert for Geri and Father Matthew, too.

6

Two hours later, we pulled my truck off the side of the road a little northeast of Pigeon Forge, and Amy pulled up behind me in her Suburban. I got out and went to the back seat to start gearing up. Amy pulled her Suburban up behind us, got out, and opened up a laptop using the hood of her SUV as a table. I loaded up a shoulder holster with my new pistol under my left arm and a couple speed loaders under my right. A paddle holster so new the leather still creaked went into the small of my back, and a brand new Taurus Judge revolver slid into it.

I grabbed a web belt with a pair of silver-edged kukris hanging from it, strapped that around my waist, then clipped a pair of spiked glove-looking things to it. The were my caestae, a Christmas gift from Amy a few years ago. They gave my hands some protection when I needed to punch above my weight class, which was almost always, and they had neat little accessories like silver and cold iron spikes, if the monster gave me time to add the appropriate accoutrements to my ensemble before starting our fight.

They almost never did, but the oversized knuckle dusters

had served me well, whether I had the spikes in or not. Something about swinging a fist the size of a Honeybaked ham wrapped in steel at someone's face can be very persuasive.

I heard an odd whirring sound coming from behind me, and turned to see a massive antenna with what looked like a collapsed umbrella on top of it rising up from the back of Amy's SUV. She tapped a few keys on her laptop and the umbrella opened up into a black mesh satellite dish, which spun around once, then pointed up at the sky toward the northwest.

"What the hell is that?" I asked. I noticed Father Matthew wince when I said "hell." He might be in for a rough time if that kind of mild swearing bothered him. Either that, or he was about to learn a whole lot of new words.

"This is a new communications rig. After your…adventure in the South Carolina swamp a few months back, I petitioned the department for a portable satellite uplink. When I expressed my belief that keeping you in more constant, consistent communication would lower the amount of property damage the government was on the hook for, they agreed that this was a far less expensive solution than letting you run around unsupervised."

"How much did that thing cost?" I asked. I was trying to figure out if I was impressed that they would spend that much money on keeping me out of trouble, or if I was offended that they thought my good behavior could be bought that cheaply.

"More than your brand-new annual salary from the Catholic Church," Amy replied.

Wow. That was more than the value of all the guns I owned, plus ammunition. Yes, I calculate my salary based on how many bullets it will buy. It's an easier system of measurement than metric, but it is subject to variance based on market forces. And hunting season. "So that thing is just going to beam Skeeter right into our heads? Did I get another implant while I was sleeping?"

Back in the day, DEMON, the super-secret predecessor to the Department of Homeland Security Paranormal Division, the moderately secret division of the federal government I currently contracted for, had implanted RFID trackers in all their agents, including me. My tracker was probably still laying in the woods between Skeeter's house and mine, having been discarded in a heavily armed disagreement I had with some former DEMON agents. Some of whom were now also formerly alive. It was a pretty serious disagreement.

Then Quincy Harker got involved, and it became a disagreement with an impressive body count. I thought I knew how to wreck shit, but that dude takes mayhem to levels I ain't even thought of.

"No, Bubba. Homeland is not interested in putting a tracker in you. They just want to put a Jiminy Cricket in your ear when you're on the clock, so maybe there's a snowball's chance you'll destroy fewer buildings," Amy said.

She handed me a little earwig communicator that didn't look any different than the ones we'd been using. I stuck it in my ear and was immediately serenaded by the dulcet tones of a middle-aged gay Black man in rural Georgia swearing about the officiating in some football game somewhere. I only follow college ball, and I root for two teams: Georgia and whoever's playing Alabama.

"Skeeter, we can hear you," I said.

"I don't give a tinker's damn whether you can hear me or not, Bubba. That call was a joke and a half, and in the biggest game of the year? I want to find that ref's eye doctor and beat his ass for him." Skeeter was way more worked up about this game than was normal for him. Frankly, the fact that he knew when the big game was happening was strange enough, much less for him to be griping about it a week and change later.

"How much do you have riding on the game, Skeet?" Geri asked as she got her little ear thingy settled.

"I've gotta do the dishes and clean the litter box for a damn month thanks to that idiot zebra and his crap eyesight!"

That made sense. Skeeter's always been pretty chill about money, knowing he can just spend some time on the computer and either earn more or fleece unsuspecting rubes in an online poker room and steal more that way. But cleaning the litter box? That one hit him where it hurt. Skeeter's boyfriend had moved in a few months back, and he brought James Tiberius Cat, a massive Maine Coon mix with a missing eye, one leg that didn't work quite right, half of one ear torn off in a fight, and a few teeth gone. That cat has seen some shit. Skeeter was pretty much in love, but J.T. Cat has not adjusted well to his new living arrangements, and Skeeter has told me horror stories about waking up to a fifteen-pound furball sitting on his chest glaring at him with the hole where his eye used to be, or J.T. Cat opening the shower curtain, taking a swipe at Skeeter's backside with his razor-sharp claws, then running away before the screaming started.

I loved the idea of Skeeter having a cat. And a boyfriend, because it had been too long. But I took a lot of joy in watching this furball turn my best friend's life completely upside down. Male friendship is often based entirely on schadenfreude. Because we're all kinda assholes.

"Lemme guess," I said. "You already do the dishes, and he snuck the cat boxes in on you when you weren't paying attention."

"We were watching the NFC Championship, and he

wanted to up the ante. I was good for it, because I was pretty sure I was gonna win, and that meant he'd be doing the dishes and my laundry for a month. But no, it's almost like somebody paid off the ref just to screw with me personally!"

"Hell, if I'd thought I could get in touch with him, I woulda paid a good bit of money to make you have to clean litter boxes, buddy," I said.

"You're a real pal, Bubba."

"Are we going to stand around talking football all night, or are we going to hunt this wampus cat?" Father Matthew asked.

Maybe he was going to be all right after all. I mean, he did give us a choice. "I reckon we didn't bring enough beer for a lengthy discussion of pro football officiating, so we might as well go hunting," I said.

"Not bringing enough beer implies that you did bring beer," Geri said.

"Yeah, there's a cooler built into the bed of the truck, and the rednecks at the hotel left all that beer behind with nobody to drink it. I dumped it into the truck and iced it down before we left."

She just shook her head and finished gearing up. I can't believe she was surprised. It's like she didn't even know me.

It took us about forty-five minutes of walking through the woods to get to the last place a wampus cat had been seen. We'd left any semblance of civilization behind half an hour ago, and couldn't even hear the highway from where we stood looking around. We were on a wooded hilltop with a clear view of at least a mile in every direction, and the setting sun had everything ablaze in brilliant oranges and golds. Geri was a good twenty feet up a live oak that was so big I couldn't even wrap my arms around it, looking for anything that looked like a wampus cat's natural habitat.

"What the hell are we looking for again?" I called up to her.

"Ponds, any kind of creek that looks deep enough for a decent-sized cat to swim in, caves, big brushfalls… Come on, Bubba. You're the Hunter. You're supposed to know this stuff."

"Skeeter's in charge of research," I replied. "I'm in charge of mayhem and alcohol."

"Play to your strengths, I guess," Father Matthew said.

I raised an eyebrow at him, and he just gave me one of those "I said what I said" shrugs that I've learned to recognize after catching a couple hundred of them from Geri over the last two years. Just what I needed—a priest who thought he had a sense of humor. "Anyhow," I called back up the tree. "You see any place that might be worth checking out?"

"Yeah, there's another big hill about half a mile west of here, and it looks like the creek carved a chunk of it away. There are some shadowy caves that might be the kind of place a wampus would like."

"How do you know which way is west?" I asked. I didn't remember her carrying a compass up the tree, and if there was a new phone app that was worth a shit at navigating the middle of nowhere, I needed that pronto.

Geri disappointed me, a little too gleefully for my tastes. She just pointed up at the setting sun. "It's over that way, where the big orange thing is falling out of the sky. I hear the sun sets in the…wait for it…west."

All my friends are smartasses. I'm not sure what that says about me, but I'm sure it says something. "Alright, then let's head west to this hill, see if there's any spots that look like they could be wampus holes, and set up a perimeter around them. Everything I've read says wampus cats are nocturnal, and ambush predators, so it'll probably be hiding until it gets dark, then come out to hunt."

Geri had been clambering down the big oak while I'd been talking, and she dropped to the ground behind me right as I finished. I turned to see her dusting the bark off her hands onto her jeans. She looked up at me and grinned. "Damn, Bubba. You sounded almost like you knew what you're doing there. Keep that up and somebody's gonna think you're a pro."

"He's just trying to impress the new boss," Skeeter said in our ears. "Nobody tell him that the Church gave us a three-year contract whether Father Matthew likes us or not."

"Ahem," Father Matthew said, looking up as though he was talking to a power much higher than my nerdy best friend. "You do know I'm on this comms channel, right?"

"Yeah," Skeeter said. "I know. I just don't care." Then he clicked off and left the four of us looking at one another in the rapidly darkening woods.

"Well, that went well," Matthew said.

"Don't sweat it, Father," Amy said, patting the slender priest on his shoulder. "Joe was more than our liaison. He was family. And for Skeeter and Bubba, he was family for their entire lives. It might take Skeeter a bit to get accustomed to someone filling his role."

Matthew nodded, his face stern. "I understand. And I don't want to take Father Joe's place. But I do have a job to do, and we can't have our tech support going off in a snit whenever he remembers that his uncle isn't the liaison any longer."

I stepped over to the priest and looked him in the eye. "Father Matthew, let me be perfectly goddamn clear. Skeeter is part of this team. He is my best friend, my brother from another mother, and one of very few people on this earth that I trust implicitly. You are none of those things. You *might* eventually become someone I trust, but Skeeter has been my best friend since middle school.

"He was there for me when my mom vanished. He stood with the family when we buried my grandparents, my brother, and my father. He was the *only* person from our part of the world who stood by me when I stuck a sword through my father's guts and watched him bleed out in front of me.

"So if anybody needs to remember anything, it's you needing to remember that we are family, whether we were born that way or not. And you ain't. Maybe not yet, maybe not ever. But if I gotta choose between losing the Church's money and their babysitter, or losing my best friend for better than twenty-five years? Well, I've survived without the Church's money before, and I reckon I can find a way to do it again. But I ain't never walked through the world as an adult without Skeeter by my side, and I don't intend to start now.

"So if you want to be part of this team, you can follow me over to that next hill and hunt some wampus. But if you want to threaten my brother because he's working through some shit, you can fuck right off." Then I stomped off through the woods to the west, not giving a shit if the priest followed me or not.

7

Spoiler alert—Father Matthew didn't follow me off into the rapidly darkening woods a few miles away from anyone who would hear him scream if I was really that pissed off at him. I wasn't. Not *really*. I was annoyed, and it was better to just lay it all out on the table early in our relationship with the new priest than to pussy-foot around stuff and have some big fight when we're in the middle of the shit and it might get us killed. If I'm gonna have to deal with team meetings and the fallout of my temper and other bullshit that I thought I was free from having to deal with by dint of not working in some big corporation, I wanna deal with that shit when nobody's actively trying to murder and/or eat me.

But it was fine that he didn't follow. Amy and Geri were back there to talk him through Dealing with Bubba 101, and I had Skeeter in my ear relaying to me anything important he picked up from being in all their ears. So I could get back to the whole purpose of the trip—hunting a flippin' wampus cat.

Now wampus cats are more than just the monster with

maybe the coolest name in creation. They're fast, deadly ambush predators, *and* they have the coolest name in creation. There's never been a recorded case of a captured wampus cat, which is why some reports say it's the size of a bobcat or a Maine coon cat on steroids, and other reports say it's the size of a mountain lion. If you aren't up on your North American predators, that's roughly the difference between a big terrier and a Great Dane, so there's a little bit of a discrepancy there.

They're also supposed to alternately be great swimmers, great climbers, incredibly fast with six legs, possessed of a long prehensile tail, and/or able to mimic human voices with their cries, luring unsuspecting hunters into the wilderness by pretending to be their wives or children. That last bit can't possibly be true, because most of the hunters I know go into the woods to escape their wives and kids, so why the hell would they follow the ankle biters anywhere? I don't have kids, so the motivations of breeders are often beyond me.

But since nobody really knows what a wampus cat looks like, and there aren't any reports of one in captivity anywhere, me and Skeeter have spent years talking about being the first people to catch a real, live wampus cat. It would make us legends in the cryptid hunting community, no matter how many damn YouTube followers Mason Dixon has. I'm not jealous. Really, I'm not. But I might be a little tired of getting compared to him just because he's the one all over the internet. I was here first, dammit.

So as I stomped through the woods, I was actually paying attention to my surroundings, not just tromping off in a huff. I remembered that the most recent sightings had all been down in valleys or hollers, and west was the more remote direction, so it made sense to head west. And since I had my earwig in, I could talk to Skeeter and he could keep track of me in case anything went sideways.

"They still arguing back there, Skeet?" I asked.

"Not as much," he replied. "Father Matthew seems to be more educated on the ways of Bubba whispering, and they're starting into the woods to follow you."

"Bubba whispering?" I asked.

"You know, when we make you think something is your idea so you'll quit bitching and go along with what needs to be done?"

"Oh yeah, that. I didn't know y'all had a name for it."

"Amy works for the government, dude. She's probably got an acronym and letterhead for it."

He wasn't wrong. My fiancée had really embraced the bureaucracy since getting hired back by the feds. And Director Pravesh was doing nothing to stem the tide of her paper-pushing, with more reports and budget forms than I'd ever seen all cascading across the top of my dining room table. I don't mind the clutter, but if the table's covered with paper, I have to find someplace else to put my empty beer cans before they go to the recycling bin under the sink, and that's a pain in the ass.

"Okay, are they following my trail, are you guiding them to me, or are they just saying 'screw it' and going off in a completely different direction?" I asked, realizing that I was standing in the middle of the woods at sunset talking to thin air. If I was hunting crazy people and came across me, I'd think I'd just bagged my limit.

"A little from column A, a little from column B," Skeeter replied. "If they stay on their current heading, they oughta catch up to you in about fifteen minutes."

Fifteen minutes? I guess I stomped off through more woods than I remember. I found a fallen tree that was kinda leaning in the crook of another pair of trees and sat down on it, testing it with my weight before finally settling all my bulk onto it, listening to the creak of the protesting wood as I did so. Everybody's a damn dietician, even in the middle of nowhere.

About ten minutes later, I heard something coming through the woods and stood up to have a look around. "Skeeter, you suck at estimating time," I said. "I can hear 'em coming through the brush already."

"Uh, Bubba," Skeeter replied. "I'm watching all four of you on my monitor. Your trackers are still half a mile apart. I don't know what's coming through the woods to you, but it's not our team."

Well, *that* got my damn attention. I looked around for cover, but it was getting hard to see in the gloom. It was dusk when I stomped off, and down here in the valley, it got dark faster than up on top of the hill. I had my pistol out, but I had limited faith in my ability to hit anything with it. It was a new gun, one that I'd only put a couple hundred rounds through, and it was coming on full night with no moon, so if I was really lucky the big boom would scare off anything coming through the woods with bad intentions. If not, well it was at least a really heavy pistol, so I could beat the shit out of something with it until they bit my arm off.

"Skeet, can you see down into this holler I'm in?" I asked.

"Not a bit," he said. "Only way I'm able to see your location is the tracker in your earpiece. Your phone isn't pinging anything, and neither are the trackers in your knives and guns."

"Well, shit," I said, then paused. "Wait, what trackers in my guns and knives?"

"The ones I planted there after you cut the tracker out of your arm." Skeeter did not sound nearly as abashed by this revelation as I wanted him to. "Oh, don't act like you give a shit about your body autonomy, Bubba. You let somebody shave a number three into your leg hair when Dale Earnhardt died."

"Yeah, but there was consent involved, Skeeter," I said. "You don't just go planting bugs in a dude's weapons. That's a serious breach of trust."

"Is it?" he asked. "How many cell phones have you smashed, thrown out of truck windows, hurled off mountaintops, chucked in lakes, or dropped in mailboxes on the side of the road, just so I'd stop bothering you?"

I thought for a second, counted on my fingers for a couple more, then said, "I don't know, ten?"

"Try thirty-seven."

"You keep count?"

"Me and Geri have a running pool each year whether you'll destroy more phones or throw more away in irritation, so I have a running tally."

"Who's winning so far?"

"Bubba, it's February."

"I know. Who's winning?"

"So far, you've only smashed one phone on the concrete this year, which is lower than your usual pace. But you also flushed one down a toilet at a rest stop, threw one off your back porch, and left one on the roof of the truck when you pulled out of the parking lot of a Buc-ee's."

"Does that count as destroyed, or lost?"

"Half credit to both," he said. "Which puts me at two and a half to Geri's one and a half."

"I reckon I better break some shit so it stays interesting."

"Bubba, if there's anything life with you can be called, it's interesting. Speaking of interesting, do you still hear something coming through the woods?"

I turned to where the sound had been coming from. "Nope," I said. "Ain't nothing coming."

"Oh, good."

"Because it's here."

"That's probably not good."

"Probably not." I looked down into the beady black eyes of one of the most dangerous predators in North America. "Skeeter, is it against the law to shoot a wild hog in Tennessee?"

This was a big pig. Like, a *big* pig. Its shoulders probably came up to my waist, and it had a pair of short tusks sticking out of its lower jaw, with a little sliver of meat still hanging from one, left over from its last meal. I was hoping that there wouldn't be little Bubba chunks hanging from it in a couple minutes.

"It's a hog?" Skeeter's voice told me that he understood exactly the danger involved. Wild hogs aren't just mean, they're mean *and* smart, with big-ass knives sticking out of their mouths. Nobody in their right mind messes with a feral pig if they've got any other choice. Unfortunately, this pig was ten feet away and glaring at me like it could smell the bacon I had for breakfast. To be fair, I went back for seconds, so maybe it *could* smell the bacon I ate fourteen hours ago. I don't know how pig noses work.

"Yeah, it's a hog," I said. "Big, bristly hair, tusks, beady eyes, looks like it wants to eat my kidneys, that kind of thing."

"You want to move very slowly," Skeeter said. "Don't startle it, but draw your pistol. If you get a chance, don't aim for the head. The skull is really thick, and I think your new hand cannon would make it through, but if you ain't dead on, it could deflect and not do anything but piss the critter off." I've noticed over the years that Skeeter sounds more country when he's scared. Which does not do wonders for the blood pressure of whoever he's on comms with when he starts to sound like a Clampett.

I did what he said, sliding my hand across my chest to pull out the massive revolver tucked under my arm. I swung the pistol around like I was moving through molasses, finally lining the front sight up with the hog's forehead. I pulled the hammer back, sending a loud *click* through the hushed wilderness, and just as I did, another three, smaller hogs came out of the underbrush.

"Well, shit," I said, decocking my gun. "Skeeter, it's a mama pig with three little babies. The babies are kinda cute, in a psychopathic, eat your innards kinda way."

"Bubba, get up a tree. Now." Skeeter's voice was tight with worry, the kind of fear I hadn't heard from him in a long time. I opened my mouth to ask him what had him so freaked out when I was forcefully reminded of exactly how intense a mother animal's instincts to defend her young could be.

Miss Piggy lowered her head, let out a snort, and charged me, her tusks aimed right at my favorite part of my anatomy. So I did what any reasonable human being would do when a wild hog charged straight at their junk.

I ran like hell.

8

I 'm not sure what made more noise crashing through the underbrush—me or the giant, murderous, ball-devouring swine. Probably me, since I was the one breaking the trail. I'm also a lot taller and a good fifty pounds heavier than the pig that was in hot pursuit. I justify my abject terror and rapid flight through the dense sticker bushes, low-hanging branches, and thick carpet of kudzu by the fact that the hog, while outweighed and outgunned, was not unarmed, as it had those razor-sharp tusks waving around in front of its face. If I had to admit my own short-comings, I'd probably also own up to the fact that the hog might have been the smarter participant in this chase, just based on the fact that I was the one running through the woods like my ass was on fire, and the pig was the one doing the chasing.

Given that this was not the time to be contemplating my poor life choices or evaluating whether or not I was smarter than a Tennessee wild hog, I just ran like hell. I stomped down saplings as I encountered them, hopped over a couple of fallen trees, vaulted a narrow creek that sluiced its way through the red dirt hillside, and finally found what I'd been desperately searching for ever since I first took flight—a climbable tree.

When you're as big as I am, you can't just climb any tree. You ain't shimmying up any narrow-ass loblolly pines once the needle crosses three hundred pounds. For one thing, you'll probably bend the whole tree slap over, which puts you right back on the ground. For another, you can't exactly wrap your legs around the trunk and dry-hump your way to safety like you're back under the bleachers with Mary Jane McGillicutty at the homecoming game, on account of you being too damned heavy. And because humping a tree hurts your nuts. Trust me. It's a long story involving Robitussin, college, and a fairy tale about dryads, but I know of what I speak.

So I needed a big tree. A *really* big tree. Preferably hardwood, and it needed to have decent-sized branches close to the ground. My vertical leap ain't what it once was, and it was barely eighteen inches before I blew out my knee. So I ran through the woods, getting my face slapped silly by branches and my clothes picked and snagged by thorns until I found a massive oak with branches both low enough and thick enough to hold my fat ass. Then I jumped for it, hauled myself up out of tusk range, and extended my middle finger to the hog, who slammed into the trunk of the tree again and again, either in frustration or in a futile effort to shake me loose. Even if the tree moved a little, I was locked onto the trunk like a tick on a hound dog, and I wasn't going any-damn-where.

The pig glared up at me again, its beady little black eyes radiating rage and hatred, then it turned and waddled off back the way we came, its bristly little butt wagging like a happy puppy at the knowledge that it had scared me off and treed me, and I wouldn't be coming back to bother its piglets. Or maybe I'm giving the pig too much credit and it didn't give a shit about me one way or another. But you spend as many years as I have running through the woods in search of things that want to murder you, and you'll anthropomorphize a little, too.

"Skeeter, do pigs hate people?" I asked the air. The air didn't answer, which was odd. That was a silly enough question that I expected Skeeter to reply almost instantly.

"Skeeter?" I called, then reached up to tap my ear, just in case a branch had somehow reached all the way inside my ear canal and turned the communicator off. My finger met nothing but flesh. Okay, flesh and a little bit of ear wax, but either way there wasn't a comm in there.

"Shit." This time I knew there wouldn't be a response, but it made me feel a little better to have my assessment of the situation out there for everyone to understand.

"SHIT!" This time I yelled it, but apparently the therapeutic effects of swearing only stretch so far, because this time I didn't feel any better. Bummer.

"GODDAMMIT!" That one was for science. I still didn't feel any better, so now that I had definitively determined that I had reached the end of profanity-based healing, I started to pat myself down and take stock of my supplies and situation.

Gun? Check. I still had the cannon in my right hand, but I paused my inventory to yank a slender pine branch out of the barrel. I slipped the pistol under my left arm and fastened the holster, then patted my right armpit and confirmed the pair of speed loaders were still there.

Backup gun? Check. My Taurus Judge revolver was nestled in the small of my back, having been clipped securely inside the waistband of my jeans. I felt some nasty scratches right where my tramp stamp would be if I had one, but my gun was still there, and I wasn't bleeding too much, so we counted that as a win. My phone was gone, having fallen out of my shirt pocket at some point in my mad dash for safety. I reckoned that might have tied up the contest Skeeter and Geri were running.

My knives were still strapped to my belt, but my caestae were gone. That one pissed me off. Amy had given me those metal-banded gauntlets for Christmas a few years back, and we'd made some improvements to them over time, adding screw-in spikes of silver, cold iron, and regular steel to handle different kinds of monsters. I kept them fastened to my belt using Velcro straps, but I must have snagged them on something as I ran, because they were nowhere to be seen. And it was getting dark, so it was getting harder and harder to see anything. I reached in my shirt pocket to turn on my phone's flashlight, then remembered that my phone was lying somewhere in a piggy footprint behind me.

"Shit." This one was more muttered than shouted, and still had absolutely no positive effects on my mental health, but at least I wasn't shouting anymore. That had to count for something, right?

I looked back up the trail I'd blazed through the forest, and started trudging back toward where I'd left the others. It was getting dark, but if I didn't lose the trail, I should be able to make it back to the rest of the team before total nightfall. I might even be able to get a spare comm from Amy, if I was lucky.

I wasn't lucky.

I not only lost the trail, I wandered so far off anything resembling a trail I couldn't swear I was still in Tennessee. I couldn't even blame it too much on the darkness, as the full moon blazed down upon me as I stood in a little clearing turning around and around trying to figure out which way might lead me back to me team and our vehicles. There was a narrow path leading off to my left, and a wider, more defined track through the woods to the right. I weighed the options and chose the right-hand path, deciding that even if I wasn't going in exactly the right direction, moving was better than sitting still where nobody had a clue how to find me, and if the way was even remotely clear, then it probably led to something resembling civilization.

Spoiler alert—it didn't.

I rumbled and stumbled through the woods for a solid hour after I lost the trail completely, tripping over vines, snapping fallen branches, and generally sounding like a grizzly bear rampaging through a Victoria's Secret. Don't ask me how I know what that sounds like—it involves a very bashful werebear and a faulty dressing room latch. Let's just say that Geri is never allowed back in the Mall of Georgia.

I finally burst out into a small clearing, just an open circle in the trees, about ten feet across. I looked up at the big old moon, shining down on me just like I was some lovestruck teenager holding hands with his sweetie, instead of a pissed-off middle-aged ex-football stud with no damn idea where his sweetie was or if he was going to be able to find her again before he rotted away in the woods forever.

"Halle-friggin'-lujah," I muttered as a shape materialized out of the gloom ahead of me. I was trying hard to rein in my potty mouth, on account of my time with Quincy Harker making me drop F-bombs like they were commas and Amy starting to make noises about meeting parents. I asked her if I could just go back to Fairyland and fight my psychotic grandparents again, but the look she gave me reminded me that Queen Mab wasn't the only terrifying woman in my life.

Standing on the far edge of the clearing was a wall. And not just a random wall, like that weird staircase in the woods on *Wynona Earp*. No, this wall was attached to other walls, and a roof, which meant there was almost certainly a whole damn building sitting there in front of me! A building that had a wisp of smoke coming up out of the chimney, a little bit of a glow peeking out through the curtains, and a damn power line running straight into it!

Yeah, in hindsight I probably should have been looking up for things like power lines instead of looking down trying to retrace my steps like I was some kind of tracker, which I ain't. My idea of hunting has always been more the "sit in a tree stand and drink beer until it ain't safe to climb down under your own power, so you spend the rest of the day just peeing on the deer rather than actually trying to shoot anything" type than the "track things through the woods like you're a mighty woodsman" type. So I didn't immediately think to look for power lines to lead me back to civilization. Not that much in that part of Tennessee was really "civilized." But I live on a mountain in Georgia, so who am I to judge?

Anyhow, this little cabin looked like it might have been the answer to all my prayers, and I was grinning like a possum as I took my first step in that direction.

That grin fell away at the unmistakable sound of somebody racking a shell into a twelve-gauge shotgun less than ten feet behind me. I turned to see a gaunt old man, shirtless, with a pair of baggy overalls swallowing his narrow frame, holding a shotgun trained on my sizable midsection. Even if I was a normal-sized person, there was no way he could shoot at that distance and not cause some serious damage.

"Who the hell are you, and what the hell are you doing skulking around behind my shitter in the middle of the night?"

That's when I noticed the man was framed in the door of a ramshackle shed. A door that stood wide open with a little crescent moon carved into it. A door that let the unmistakable aroma of outhouse waft through the crisp night air and assault my nostrils with its funk.

Well, at least the old fart had pulled his britches up before threatening to kill me. I raised my hands up over my head and uttered the words that so many men have uttered, and so few situations have been helped by.

"I can explain."

9

I t didn't take much more explaining past "I'm lost as shit" before the old guy took the shotgun off his shoulder and pointed toward the back wall of his house.

"Come on, let's at least have a drink while we figure out where you think you're trying to be, and how that dragged your sorry ass to my back yard where you interrupted an old man and his nightly constitutional."

I noticed he didn't throw the scattergun over his shoulder, just pointed it less directly at me. He could still swing it up and cut me in half in a fraction of the time it would take me to charge him and steal his...I dunno, outhouse? But I went where he pointed, being the one without a gun in my hands at the moment.

He guided me around the back wall to the front of the cabin, a small place maybe thirty feet on a side. Not much by city standards, but if it was just me living way out in the woods, I could totally see living in something that size. Skeeter wouldn't survive. He takes up more space than that just with comic books and vintage toys.

The old man directed me up onto the porch, where a mini-fridge sat between two rocking chairs. I took one, slowly settling my weight into it until I was sure it would hold. That's something you learn being one of the biggest people you know—most things aren't built to accommodate you. I've never had a shower in a hotel bathroom that I didn't have to bend down to wash my hair in, I've turned more than one plastic lawn chair into shrapnel, and the last time I was on a commercial airplane, there were multiple seat belt extenders required for me to comply with FAA regulations. There are some issues that go along with being a big dude, but as long as I'm willing to stay fat, I can eat all the cheese I want, so I reckon I'm just going to pay attention to the weight limit stickers on ladders forever.

"Now what the hell are you doing wandering around out here in the Tennessee mountains in the dark?" he asked, reaching into the mini-fridge and pulling out two cans of Budweiser. I usually prefer something ever so slightly higher shelf than Bud, but crappy beer is better than no beer, and it wasn't Milwaukee's Best, so I kept my mouth shut except to drink.

I pondered how much to tell the old guy. I'm pretty open about my career to most folk. Either they don't believe me, so they just think I'm making something up and can't talk about whatever secret crap I'm doing, or the believe me and can't wait to tell me about that time their Great-Aunt Lulabelle saw a ghost flitting around in her laundry one night, but it turned out to just be the perky gym teacher peeping in their cousin Clarabelle's window while she put on her pjs.

"If you're taking all this time to make up a lie, it better be good, son," he said after a long slurp of his beer.

I figured I might as well tell him the truth, or at least part of it. "I'm out here hunting a wampus cat," I said. "I work for the government, and we've gotten reports of the creature damaging property and maybe endangering people, so we need to see if it really is a cryptid, and if so, whether or not we need to rehome it or put it down."

"Rehome? Put it down?" The old man looked at me with wide eyes. "Boy, are you saying that the United States Government—" except he said it more like Youuuunited States Gubmint "—has a whole department dedicated to hunting down monsters?"

"A couple, actually," I said. "I work for the Department of Homeland Security, and we handle most domestic cryptic and paranormal threats, but there are also departments that handle strictly international issues, as well as one division within the National Park Service that takes care of any incursions into our parks and monuments. They also manage Jurassic Park."

"They what the what?"

"It's the nickname we have for the Cryptic Preserves the government has scattered around the country. You know, Area 51, Area 52, Area 69, those places."

He looked dubious. "I've heard of Area 51, but them other two…"

I laughed. "Yeah, okay, I made up Area 69. The cryptic preserves started numbering with 50, but there's only 15 of them, so there is no Area 69. *That I know of*, I mentally corrected. The federal government has a lot of money, and a fetish about secrets, so for all I knew there was an Area 69 out there somewhere, I just didn't know shit about it.

"So you're some kind of federal agent?" I nodded. "You got ID?"

I reached in my back pocket and pulled out my credentials. He leaned over and took them from my hand, then fished a pair of reading glasses out of the bib on his overalls. He peered through the cheaters at my badge, then passed it back.

"Says you're a contractor," he said. "That like Blackwater for monsters or something?"

"Nothing like that," I said. "I mean, I'm a government contractor, but not a psycho like those guys. I also work for the Catholic Church. Kinda double-dipping, really, since the same jobs often end up doing work for both groups, but a man's gotta make a living, you know?"

He relaxed a little when I mentioned the Church, which was good. It was always a little dicey, mentioning Catholics in the rural South. It certainly isn't the predominant denomination down here, and the less people are exposed to other groups of people, the more their ignorance tends to bubble up. This old guy was either progressive for a hermit, or he just didn't have a problem with Catholics. Either way was fine with me.

"You got ID for that, too?"

"Nah, the Vatican doesn't send out badges. I think they want us to be more incognito."

"They might wanna think about hiring somebody that don't blot out the whole damn sun when they walk through a clearing, then." He laughed and pulled out another pair of beers. I chugged the last of mine and took the proffered can.

We sat there in a companionable silence for a while, just listening to the cicadas and the trickle of water from a creek off to our left. After I finished my second beer, I stood up. "I think I gotta go borrow your outhouse, friend."

"Oogy," the old man replied.

I stopped, my bladder completely forgotten in my concern that this old hermit picked now to have a stroke. "Excuse me?" I asked. "Are you alright?"

"Yeah, I'm fine," he said. "Why wouldn't I be?"

"You just made this weird noise. Sounded like you said 'boogie,' apropos of nothing at all."

He threw his head back and laughed, which, while

confusing, was a little comforting, too. If he was *compos mentis* enough to think I was an idiot, he was probably not having a stroke, or at least not much of one. "Boy, you make me laugh like that again, we gonna be racing for that shitter. My name's Oogy, not 'boogie.' You called me friend, so I figured I might as well tell you my name so you could just use that instead."

"Oh," I said, feeling about as stupid as he must have thought I was. "Well…Oogy, my name's Bubba."

He raised an eyebrow. "Bubba? Your ID says Robert. What's the matter? Your kid brother couldn't say 'Bobby' when he was little?"

Well, that was a kick right in the junk. Because Oogy was right. I went by Bubba on account of some speech issues my kid brother Jason had when he was growing up. He had issues with 'y' sounds, so he called me Bubba. It stuck, even after me and Jace grew apart. And it doesn't grow much further apart than one of you being on the right side of the dirt, and the other one buried in it. I killed my brother Jason when he went nuts and tried to raise a cryptid army to take over the world. If he'da just wanted Georgia, we might could worked something out, but the whole world? Nah, that didn't fly.

So yeah, my younger brother, who was now dead by my hand, was the reason I was called Bubba, and out here in the middle of nowhere, Tennessee, separated by my team and my loved ones, was not where I wanted to be when it was time to dredge all that up and sift through it. So I didn't. I just got up without answering, walked around to the outhouse, relieved myself of some Bud Light, and came back a few minutes later, hoping Oogy would have forgotten about his queston or taken the hint that I didn't feel like answering.

I rejoined Oogy on the porch and said, "Think I can use your phone to call my team?"

"Sure," he said. "Soon as the battery's charged enough to make a call. Been dead a few days." He held up an ancient flip phone. "Only damn way I can get the telemarketers to quit calling me for a free estimate on new siding for my house!" He cackled with laughter, and after a moment, I joined in. The cabin was full-on log construction, without any place to put siding. This thing had obviously been built decades ago, when people were way more concerned about protection from the elements than about being able to get the perfect shade of eggshell on their siding to go with their royal blue shutters. Geri's been on an HGTV kick, so I've gotten a lot of strange additions to my vocabulary lately.

I looked around the porch and didn't see any outlets, which surprised me not a bit. My own cabin is at least half a century newer than this one, and I don't have receptacles on my front porch, either. If I put in places for people to charge their phones, they might stay longer. And there ain't many people that I want at my cabin at all, much less for a protracted stay. "You need me to go inside and plug it in for you?" I asked.

"Nah," he said. "Lost the charger about six months ago. Ain't made it back to town to get a new one yet."

I stared at him, open-mouthed, for at least a minute before the old bastard threw his head back and laughed that big belly laugh again. "I got you, son! You probably believe the check really is in the mail and that she'll still respect you in the morning."

I had to laugh along with him. "Nah," I said, mimicking his earlier response. "I ain't lookin' for respect, just some-where warm to lay my…head." I gave him a conspiratorial wink, and we both chuckled.

Oogy stood up, stretched, and opened the door into the house. "Come on in," he said. "I didn't lose the charger, but the phone *is* deader than hell. Might as well stay warm while we wait for it to get enough juice to make a call. Besides, I could go for something a little more stout than beer."

"As long as it ain't peach schnapps," I said. "I think I got a little PTSD from the last time I drank that shit."

"Son, I got a little PTSD just thinking about drinking that shit," the old man said with a laugh. Then we went into his cabin, where the real drinking started.

10

B ubba, how the ever-loving hell do you manage to find a way to get drunk no matter where we go for a case?" Geri asked the next morning.

I held up a finger. "One, I am a very talented man, and finding booze where there should not be booze is but one of those talents. Two, please stop shouting. I have a little bit of a headache."

"He means he's hungover as a dog," Oogy said from where he puttered around the small kitchen, then cut loose one of those laughs that felt so light and fun the night before, but felt like someone driving a spike right through my left eye this morning.

"We know what it means, Mr. Pierce," Amy said, giving me one of the death glares she's perfected in the years we've been together. I'm pretty sure she didn't even have an "injure" glare, or a "severely maim" glare before we started dating, but now she's working her way past death glare and all the way to a "murder you and everyone you've ever spoken to" glare. I bring out the best in people.

"Please, sweet cheeks, call me Oogy," he said as he

deposited a plate full of bacon with four slices of buttered toast in front of me. I put a light sprinkle of garlic salt on the toast and tucked in with gusto, ignoring the stunned looks from everyone in the room. A lot of people don't want to eat when they're hung over, but I've always found that recovery meals are important for Olympic-level drinking, just like any strenuous exercise. My recovery meal just involves fried pork products and garlic. I mean, I was sweating cheap domestic beer and Wild Turkey, so it ain't like I was smelling fresh as a daisy in the first place.

Amy was standing frozen by the old man passing out food and calling her "sweet cheeks." I knew what happened to the last guy who called her that, because I *am* the last guy that called her that. She beat my ass in unarmed combat practice, then took over our cardio workouts and ran me until I puked every other day for two weeks. And that's not even counting how long I slept on the couch. But Oogy was an old man, and a little bit charming, in a backwoods, crotchety kind of way, so maybe she wouldn't put him in traction.

"Oogy," she said, her voice so sweet butter wouldn't melt in her mouth. "If you call me sweet cheeks, dumpling butt, cutie pie, or any other comment on my appearance or femininity again, I'm going to have the IRS crawl all over your existence for the rest of your life. I will have them audit you within an inch of your life, then put a lien on any assets you have, had had, or will ever have. Are we clear?"

Oogy gave her a rakish grin. "One hundred percent, apple bottom. I will not make any comment about how you're almost as hot as Raquel Welch, or that your bulletproof vest does nothing to hide the fluid dynamics experiment you got going on under that t-shirt. I won't even talk about how cute the dimples are on your cheeks, and I certainly won't make any assumptions about any dimples you might have on your other cheeks." Then he set a heaping plate of eggs and bacon down in front of her, along with a tall glass of orange juice, and turned back to the stove.

Amy was, in a word, speechless. It was the first time I'd seen her like that in a long time, and it took everything I could do, including shoveling bacon into my face as hard and fast as I could, to keep from falling out of my chair laughing. Even Geri grinned as she leaned over and said in a whisper loud enough to be heard halfway to Florida, "I think he's fucking with you, Boss."

Amy just grinned and took a sip of her OJ. "Yeah, and I think he won that round, too. Mr. Pierce, did Bubba tell you anything about why we're here, or did he just get drunk on your porch?"

"Yeah, he said something about hunting a wampus cat. Sounded like a crock to me, but we was already drinking by that point, so I let it slide. So what are y'all doing up here? Revenuers don't come down from old Rocky Top, you know."

"Despite the song, Mr. Pierce, we aren't revenuers. We work for the government, but we could care less about any stills we might find."

"Hold on now," I said. "I'm real interested in stills."

"We aren't robbing bootleggers, Bubba." Amy didn't even look at me, just threw that one out without missing a beat. "Mr. Pierce, we've had reports of wampus sightings in the area, and they're not only increasing, but moving closer and closer to populated areas. While we don't have any direct experience with wampus cats ourselves, we have far too much experience with what happens when cryptids meet up with humans without any protections for either group."

"A lot of people or critters end up dead," I said.

"So what do you want from me?" Oogy said. He gestured to a massive gun safe. "I got my shooting irons all cleaned and ready to go, but I ain't as young as I once was. Might not be the best choice for a local guide these days."

I could tell that admission pained him a little. Some men don't take to aging well at all. My grandfather was like that. He hunted until the day he died, finally falling to a nest of vampires when I wasn't good enough to save him. He was first on the list of family members whose deaths were my fault. I wished his name was the whole list, but it wasn't even close.

"Honestly, we were just hoping to retrieve Bubba and get him out of your hair," Geri said. "The fact that you made breakfast is a huge bonus. *Somebody* booked us at a Fairfield, completely ignoring the fact that their idea of a Continental breakfast is a cup of yogurt and stale bagels."

Father Matt at least had the good grace to look ashamed of his choice of hotels. I kinda wished I'd been able to sleep in a Fairfield in bed the night before. All Oogy had was a hammock strung up between a couple of the posts on his porch. Better than nothing, but still pretty damn sketchy when you're as big as I am and as drunk as I was when I finally tried to situate myself for sleeping.

I never did make it work and ended up just sleeping on the grass with the hammock bunched up under my head for a pillow. Not even in the Top Ten worst places I'd ever slept.

"But if you have any information on the wampus and its movements, we would, of course, appreciate it," Amy said, sliding that in there all smooth like a real government official. Look at my girl, sounding all professional and shit. She totally didn't learn any of that running around with me and Skeeter.

"I reckon if y'all were really interested in finding a wampus cat, you could go check out where them city boys are building a new theme park about five miles northeast of here. I hear tell there's been some equipment getting wrecked, and even a couple of night watchmen getting mauled by mountain lions they ain't never seen."

"If they were ambushed by a mountain lion, it's more likely they would have been found in pieces, not in a hospital," Father Matt said. "They're frequently the apex predator of any environment they're found in, and they do not take kindly to having their habitats disturbed. I can't imagine two attacks both leaving survivors." That fit with what I knew about mountain lions, so I let the skinny new priest keep going.

"From the reports we have been able to verify, wampus cats are smaller than mountain lions, a little larger than the average bobcat, and much less likely to continue to attack humans once they no longer pose a threat to their environment," he continued.

"What he means is, a wampus cat ain't gonna drag your carcass home to its den and feed your kidneys to its kittens," I translated, just in case Oogy didn't deal well with the pontificating Father Matt was doing.

"I got that, son," Oogy replied. "I went to college before you was even born. Just because I live back in the woods don't mean I've always been a backwoods redneck."

"If only the same could be said for everyone in this room," Geri muttered under her breath.

"I heard that," I grumbled at her.

"I meant for you too," she replied.

"Anyway," Amy cut us off before we could start into "she's touching me" and "I wanted the window seat." She glared at the two of us, to no effect, then turned her attention back to Oogy. "Could you show me on a map where this construction is taking place? I expect we could find it, but with Bubba in the driver's seat, the more specific we can be, the better."

She pulled a tablet out of her backpack and plopped it onto the table. I rescued the last of the bacon from the ignominious fate of getting cold and being ignored by popping it into my mouth and crunching it down with a contented smile.

Geri glared at me. "You know that was my plate, right?"

"Key word there is 'was,' young Paduan," I replied.

"Don't try to get all Jedi master on me, Bubba," Geri said. "You might have the beard turning gray, but the only thing strong with you is gas."

Before I could formulate a decent comeback, Amy straightened up and tossed a wadded-up bundle of fabric to me. I shook it out and a black t-shirt unfurled, with a stick of deodorant clattering to the table. "I brought your truck, so go out and put that on," she said. "I don't want to ride anywhere with you smelling like cheap beer and bad decisions."

"God, Boss," Geri said, laughing. "Cheap beer and bad decisions is practically Bubba's natural musk. If you don't want him smelling like that, he's gonna have to ride in the bed of his own truck."

Deciding that everyone was a damned comedian this morning, I took my faded Giggletime Mountain Amusement Park t-shirt and my Old Spice out into the morning sun to wipe away at least one layer of yesterday's funk. I had peeled off my dirty shirt, admitting to myself that it didn't exactly smell daisy-fresh, when I heard someone clear their throat behind me.

"What is it, Padre?" I asked.

"I just wanted to make sure we're all on the same page, Bubba," he said, his voice a little tenuous.

"We hunt monsters, the Church pays me a bunch of money," I said. "I don't know as how there's many more pages to be on, are there?"

"I'm not trying to replace Father Joseph—"

"Don't worry." I cut him off with a wave of my hand. I

turned back and looked him in the eye, only possible because he was standing on one of the porch steps. "Ain't no chance of that." I turned back to the new liaison. "Look, Father Matt. I expect you're a good dude. Dedicating your life to the service of something bigger than you is a good thing, and being willing to go out in the woods with a bunch of heavily armed government contractors to hunt down monsters that most folk don't even believe exist says that you've got a pair of brass balls to go along with that good heart. But you ain't family."

I kept going. "Joe was more than just Skeeter's adopted uncle. He wasn't much older than we were, so he was as much a big brother to us as anything. He looked out for us when we were little, he taught me how to smoke cigarettes we stole from my daddy's dresser, he even helped me pass freshman algebra. Ain't no way you can fill the hole in our lives that Joe left. That don't mean we can't make space for you on our team, or in this weird-ass little family we done built here. But you're gonna have to do it your way. Not Joe's way, not the Church's way, and sure as hell not the federal government's way. Just…relax a little bit. You're here, and we ain't tied you up and thrown you in the back of the truck for three days like we did the one 'interim liaison' we had for a week the one time Uncle Joe went on vacation and we had to hunt down a pack of were-donkeys in Alabama. Just give us some time and we'll probably come around to accepting you. You ain't ever gonna be Joe, but if you work at it, you might be a pretty damn good Matt."

The little priest looked at me for a long minute, then nodded and stuck out his hand. "Thanks for that. I'll work on it."

We shook, and he nodded toward my torso. "But you should put a shirt on. I think I did hear a mountain lion as we were looking for you in the woods last night, and with as hairy as you are, I'd hate for one to mistake you for a possible mate."

I laughed and finished changing, and the others joined us at the trucks to continue our hunt. Oogy said goodbye to everyone, then stood by the door of my pickup with his hand out. "I like you, kid. You remind me a little bit of my grandson. You don't have an unhealthy obsession with old video games and NASCAR, do you?" he asked as I clasped his hand.

"I still play Mario Brothers on my original SNES, Oogy. If it's got more than sixteen bits, I ain't interested."

"Yeah, that's like my boy. Y'all got a lot in common. Good kids, but y'all need a shave. You take care now, alright?"

"You too, old man," I said, smiling as I slid behind the wheel. "You too."

I looked at the team, gathered around Amy's Suburban and my F-250 and said, "Let's go do what we do."

"Get shitfaced drunk and beat up rednecks in bars?" Geri asked as Father Matt looked horrified.

"Nah, that's Tuesdays. This is Thursday. That's hunt monsters *then* get drunk and beat up rednecks in bars," I said.

Geri and I high-fived as Amy grinned and Father Matt gave us yet another "what have I gotten myself into" stares. It was wampus-hunting time!

11

Another day, another hungover monster hunter rolling up to a construction site that's the likely cause of a bunch of cryptid or paranormal crap. One of these days, I'll learn to just start my hunt at the nearest cluster of bulldozers and dickheads with hardhats. And sure enough, I had just put one foot down on the red dirt outside the largest and least rundown trailer on the site when a young guy with a white hard hat and a paisley necktie came rushing up to the side of my truck with his hands waving over his head like he was trying to direct flights at LaGuardia.

"You can't be here!" he hollered, despite being less than ten feet away from my damn face. "This is a closed site, and no one is allowed here without the proper permits. Now turn this hunk of junk around and get to steppin'!"

Now I'll put up with a lot in my line of work. I've traipsed through cow pastures dodging bovine land mines at three in the morning. I've almost burned down a shopping mall lighting fairies on fire. Shit, I even went to a ballet once on a hunt. But I will not stand idly by while some snot-nosed pencil neck who only has to shave every third day insults my truck.

But I had promised Amy that I would do everything in my power not to get arrested this time. So I didn't slap the little weenie into the middle of next week. I just reached in my back pocket, held up my credentials, and said, "I think this counts as my permit. Now you apologize to my truck before I start looking for OSHA violations."

I gave him my best "don't mess with me" glare, which was pretty good now that I was out of the truck and able to stretch to my full height. He was a tall drink of water himself, only a couple inches shorter than me, but about a foot less in diameter, and I did have a very large fashion accessory hanging from a holster under my left arm, an accessory that Foreweenie definitely noticed, based on how big around his eyes got. He almost skidded to a stop, he halted his power walk toward me so fast.

"Um, uh, I…"

"It's okay, Mr.…?" Amy slid out of her Suburban and walked around to the now-frozen foreweenie. "We're with the Department of Homeland security and wanted to come check out some reports of vandalism to nearby businesses. We want to see if any of your equipment has been tampered with while the site was empty."

Foreweenie now looked more confused than terrified, which I didn't think was an upgrade. He turned around in a complete circle. "Nearby businesses? What kind of fake news revenuer bullshit is that? There ain't so much as a gas station for five miles in every direction. Now how about you tell me why you're really here, Missy. And don't give me none of your deep state propaganda, neither. I want the real truth!"

Wow. I just spent the night with a geriatric mountain man who looked like he should be singing "God Bless the U.S.A." at the top of his lungs at a political rally, but he was as mellow and pleasant an individual as I could have hoped to meet. Now here I was, just a few miles away, staring at the Great White Hope - Conspiracy Theorist Edition. I almost wanted to hold him down and vaccinate him, just to see if he'd burst into flames.

Amy, however, was slightly more mature than me. Slightly. Because she did have buttons, and apparently an officious little prick calling her "Missy" at ten in the morning pressed a lot of them. She walked up to Foreweenie and put a hand on his shoulder. She leaned in close, until they were almost touching foreheads, and said, "I'll tell you this, you inbred, backwoods piece of shit. If you ever want to get on a female Deputy Director of Homeland Security's good side, and trust me, that is the side you want to be on, calling her 'Missy' is not how you get there. Now let's start again, and I'll pretend I wasn't just insulted by a misogynistic putz and you'll pretend you *aren't* a misogynistic putz. How does that sound?"

I gave my best stage whisper, which is only about five decibels below my maximum shouting voice, and said, "I'd take her up on that, pal. I can see three different violations from here that'll get you shut down for at least a week, and I ain't even started looking."

He spluttered, looking from Amy to me, then back to Amy, and after a long moment where I wondered if I was going to be called upon to back up my totally fabricated accusation of OSHA violations with fact, he deflated. Like, almost literally. His puffed-up little chest sank in on itself, his face fell all the way to the basement, and he even shrank a couple inches in height, like if he was using pump up lifts in his shoes and they just had a blowout. Now I want to market a new kind of shoe that pumps up to make you taller. I bet Tom Cruise would buy the patent for a billion dollars.

Anyway, Foreweenie shrank in on himself at the sight of a

strong woman with a badge and gun, and said, in a meek voice, "What can I do for y'all today?"

"That's better," Amy said, folding her badge wallet and tucking it away in a back pocket. "Now—"

"Hold up," I said, taking my life in my hands by interrupting the woman who knew both where I slept and where I kept all my knives. "You still owe somebody an apology." I nodded toward my truck.

Foreweenie gaped at me. "Are you serious?"

I glared down at him, a lot easier since he shrank even further. He kept this up he was going to be short enough to audition for that new *Lord of the Rings* show. "Do I look like somebody who ever jokes about my truck?"

He gulped and said, "I'm sorry, truck." It obviously pained him to say it, like the words stuck in his throat a little. I thought about continuing to screw with him, making him do it again and again until I was satisfied that he was appropriately penitent, but a look at Amy's expression put the brakes on that idea. So I just waved at her to continue.

"As I was saying," she said, in a tone that promised at least a weak on a lumpy couch or in Skeeter's guest room, "we have had reports of wild animal attacks in the area, and we wanted to see if you've had any strange occurrences here at the site."

Foreweenie looked around, like he was now afraid to be seen talking to us. He didn't have much to worry about, since there were only three vehicles in the parking lot: my truck, Amy's Suburban and his white Prius. Seriously, a Prius? He was talking shit about my truck, and he was driving a *Prius?* Nobody was ever going to take this dude seriously on a construction site with those wheels. Hell, I had enough trouble getting them to listen to me, and that's just because I drove a truck that wasn't generic contractor white.

"Come into the office. I don't want to talk about it out

here. The guys might be back from lunch soon." He turned and practically scurried up the steps to the job site trailer. We all exchanged confused glances and followed him. I brought up the rear so I could take one last look around, just in case there happened to be a wampus cat wandering through the middle of a wide-open construction site in the middle of the day. There wasn't, but there did seem to be a narrow trail winding its way through the woods off to the east of the site.

We crowded into the small office at the back of the trailer, with Foreweenie sitting behind the messy desk in a rolling chair that had the arms held together with silver duct tape. Pretty easy to see where this guy lived in the corporate power structure. Geri grabbed a folding chair from around the folding "conference table" that took up most of the main part of the trailer, and planted herself behind and between Amy and Father Matt, making a little triangle while I leaned against the far wall. I picked my spot both on account of there not being but two guest chairs and on account of wanting to keep glaring down at this dude a little longer.

"Is the door closed? Would you lock it, please?" Foreweenie looked up at me with something like actual fear in his eyes.

"No," I said, my voice flat. "Now what the hell has got you so shook? You came on like a house afire, all regulations this and closed site that, but the minute the Deputy Director mentioned weird critters, you started looking like a long-tailed cat in a rocking chair factory." Yeah, I know my metaphor fell apart a little with the modification, but I was trying something new.

He slumped back in his chair and let out a long breath, redolent of onions, oil, and vinegar. I could see the telltale sub sandwich wrapper sticking out of his wastebasket, with what looked like a dab of mayo on one corner. Ugh. Mayo's disgusting, and I can't fully trust anybody that would pick that to go on a sandwich in a world where mustard and hot sauces exist. That long sigh moved some papers off a stack at the front of his desk, and as Amy reached out to save them from cascading to the floor, I noticed one of those gold desk nameplates that bankers and officious construction foremen have on their desks.

Anthony Gerald Cooper. That was Foreweenie's real name. I don't think it was noticeably better than "Foreweenie," but I tried to make it stick, at least until I could get out of the trailer and forget this idiot ever existed. "There have been some strange occurrences on the site. Equipment being damaged, strange tracks around the trailer after it rained, weird sounds coming from the woods at night. I went through five different security guards, but none lasted more than two days. I finally started spending a few nights a week out here myself, and there's definitely something in those woods, and it does *not* like us being here."

"When did the trouble start, Mr. Cooper?" Amy asked. I looked around for a second to see who she was talking to, then remembered that Foreweenie's name was right there in front of me. Guess I was faster at forgetting him than I expected to be.

12

Tony, which was what Foreweenie preferred to be called, told us his tale of wrecked equipment, strange noises, and tracks that looked like no animal he'd ever seen. I traded glances with Amy and Geri, thinking that this city slicker probably hadn't seen much of anything past the tracks of the wild Nike and Reebok, but I let it go. Then he walked us out to a shed behind the job trailer and unlocked a heavy padlock.

He looked around again, making sure the whole site was deserted before pulling open the door and showing us a mangled mass of steel and aluminum. Before I could even start to decipher what the mess started life as, he gestured to it, his voice going up an octave in his excitement or terror. I couldn't really tell which.

"See?" he said, pointing all over the inside of the shed at twisted bars, pretzeled wire mesh, and snapped chains. "This thing has destroyed every trap I've set for it!"

Okay, now that I knelt down and got a good look, these had been traps at some point in their life. A couple looked like the humane catch-and-release traps that animal shelters and vets loan out for people to trap stray dogs and cats and have them neutered. One looked like a homemade rabbit trap, but big enough to hold a German Shepherd, and another chunk of twisted wrought iron was unmistakable once I saw the massive spring and the nasty jaws.

"You used a bear trap? In public woods?" I turned on the little foreman, ready to punch his lights out. He could have seriously hurt an innocent person walking through the woods, or worse, snapped an animal's leg and left it out there to suffer. I might be a hunter, both of monsters and meat, but I've never been into making animals suffer. That kind of crap gives rednecks a bad name, and we don't need any help.

"No." Tony held up both hands and took a step back. "I used a bear trap on land that was clearly marked No Trespassing, far from any houses or businesses, where the only thing close was our job site and whatever was wrecking our stuff." He pointed to a pile of shredded hoses, shattered glass, and other detritus piled in a corner of the shed. "That's what's left after the thing got hold of my pickup. Busted every piece of glass on the thing, slashed all four tires, ripped off the tailgate, and twisted the hood up into a ball."

Now that I shone my flashlight onto the pile of crap farther back in the shed, I could make out the beginning of the word "Toyota" on a twisted white rectangle. I let out a soft chuckle. Next time he oughta buy a Ford.

"Let me take a look at this," Father Matt said, slipping past me into the small room. He picked up the twisted mesh that had once been a humane trap and turned it over in his hands. He plucked a few strands of hair from it and passed it over to me. "What do you think this looks like, Bubba?" he asked.

I took the little ball of fluff, which was way softer than I expected from a horrific forest monster with the strength to tear metal apart. It was gray and downy, like a dog's undercoat, or like…

"Holy shit," I said, looking at the priest.

"Yeah, that's what I thought," Matt replied.

"You wanna share with the rest of the class?" Geri asked from outside the shed.

"Just a sec," I said, kneeling by Matt's side and looking where he pointed. There were little flecks of a dark brown substance that could only be dried blood, and bigger drops on the barely recognizable bear trap. "They caught something," I said, looking at Matt.

"A couple of somethings," he agreed.

"And Mama got *pissed*."

"Mama?" Amy's voice had a little more behind it than just a question, because if this wampus cat had wampus kittens, our job just got a lot harder and a *lot* more dangerous. As I learned again last night, nothing will fight harder than a mother defending her babies, and when that mother has claws, maybe a spiked ball on her tail, and the strength to bend steel…well, let's just say stepping up to a pissed-off Mama Wampus was not at the top of my bucket list. It was even further down than getting chased through the woods by a pissed-off Mama Boar, and I knew intimately how much fun that wasn't.

Matt and I stood and turned back to the trio waiting for us outside the shed. Matt looked at me, but I waved for him to go on. After all, he figured it out, so he oughta get to share the good news with everybody.

"Bad news," he said. "It seems that our wampus cat has at least one kit, probably more. The fur we found caught in the cage was very soft, like a baby animal's first coat. And there was a little blood on the remnants of the cage, which may have come from the kit injuring itself trying to escape, or it may be from the mother rescuing its baby."

"Who could blame her?" Geri asked, shooting a dark look at Tony. She liked all animals, and not many people, so the use of a bear trap had left a nasty taste in her mouth where the little foreman was concerned. Tony wisely kept his mouth shut.

"How long ago did you find this trap all jacked up?" I asked.

"About two weeks ago," he replied.

"Great. That means that Mama Wampus is probably all healed up and rarin' to get her revenge on the nasty two-legged hairless cats who hurt her baby and her leg. Fantastic." I tapped the comm unit in my ear. "Skeeter, you got any reports of other property damage within a two-mile radius of this site?"

"Bubba," Skeeter came back seconds later. "There ain't even any property within two miles of this site. If it wasn't for this amusement park, there wouldn't be any people for ten miles in any direction."

Now it made sense, in a greedy robber baron asshole kind of way. I could see it now—this wasn't about building an amusement park; this was about building a whole town. The developer probably bought up all the woods for miles around, and was planning on cutting a bigger road, adding hotels, apartments for staff, restaurants, and shopping for visitors and employees. Owning a piece of all that would give him a nice diverse investment opportunity for venture capitalist assholes to chop down a bunch more trees for yet another friggin' water slide. I hate water slides. There was an unfortunate swim trunk incident at Elizabeth Bruno's tenth birthday party that left me a little hydrophobic. And not the kind you get when a stray bat bites you, which happens way more often than you want in my line of work. Lucky for me, my part-fairy blood keeps me from getting most mundane diseases.

"So how big are the plans for the rest of the site?" I asked. "Show me."

Tony opened his mouth to protest, but I tapped the butt of my pistol at the same time Amy cleared her throat and held up her badge wallet, and all his arguments were suddenly invalid. He locked up the shed, then led us back into the trailer where he opened the bottom drawer of a flat file cabinet and pulled out a set of blueprints with CONFIDENTIAL stamped on the cover sheet in huge red letters. "Please don't tell anyone I showed you these. I could lose my job and be sued over breaking my NDA."

"National Security, Mr. Cooper," Amy said. "My badge trumps any NDA you've ever signed."

So does my gun, I thought. But for once, I managed to avoid saying it. I'm trying to learn to take the win with my mouth shut. It ain't easy.

Tony laid the massive sheaf of papers onto the top of the flat file and started flipping through. There had to be two hundred plates in that stack, more than I'd ever seen on a set of construction documents before. Admittedly, the blueprints I'm used to looking at are either stuff I drew on the back of a napkin to explain how I wanted to rebuild my bathroom (Amy wouldn't let me, no matter how many times I promised her an indoor jacuzzi), or they're plans for a building I'm trying to break into, and I usually just make Skeeter steal those so he feels like he's got something to do. We all know I'm just going to kick the door down anyway, no matter what the plans say.

"The initial scope of the project is the park and the access roads, but the plan is to lay in the infrastructure for a much larger community, including homes, retail, and other entertainment options. Our vision is—"

"Tony, we don't give a shit," I interrupted the little dude before he could get going. "We just need to see the big site plan. What I think you middle management nerds call the twenty-thousand-foot view."

Tony's face fell, and you woulda thought I'd just insulted his truck. But since his truck was a twisted pile of metal, and a Toyota, there wasn't a whole lot left to insult. "Oh. Right. Sorry, it's just been a while since I was able to talk to anyone about the scope of the project."

He flipped a few more pages, then stepped back and gestured to the cabinet. "That's the overall site plan, showing the boundaries of the park, with retail and restaurants centered around the southern edge, hotels along the northern side, and housing to the west. We plan to construct a six-lane highway leading directly from Pigeon Forge to here, passing through all the shopping areas en route to the park."

I pointed at several of the locations to the west, then tapped my comm again. "Skeeter, you still got that camera hidden in the butt of my gun?" I asked.

"Yeah, that's one of them. I've got a cam in Amy's necklace, too, so I've got a pretty good view of the plans," he replied.

I tried hard not to think about all the other places he could have planted cameras. Not only did he have a key to my cabin, he had more access to it than I did. He set up my whole smart home system, so if Skeeter wanted to take control of my house, he wouldn't even have to leave his recliner. "Do the places I'm tapping on this blueprint line up with that arc of confirmed sightings Father Matt showed us?"

"Gimme a second," he said. I could hear tapping as he did some kind of computery thing I neither understood nor cared about. "Yep," he said after a few seconds. "Those housing areas are exactly where the earlier wampus sightings took place."

I looked up at Tony. "Lemme guess. Y'all already started building temp housing for the crew, and they're all staying right around here, aren't they?"

Tony looked confused. "Yeah, but how could you tell that?"

"Because I'm a Hunter, dumbass. Not just monsters, but deer, rabbit, squirrel, and anything else that'll go in a pot. When y'all started building housing, you disturbed the wampus cat's natural habitat. So it ran away from the noisy humans and their noisy machines. Then you followed them, chasing them from spot to spot as you graded sites, dug sewer lines and septic tanks, and all that shit. They kept running east, and y'all kept getting closer."

I leaned in and pointed to a line of blue running along the eastern edge of the development site. "That's your boundary, isn't it? That river?"

"Yeah, that's where our project stops. The final plan is luxury river homes, once we've made the whole area a destination." Tony's chest puffed out a little. He was obviously proud of his work.

I almost hated to deflate him, but I did it anyway. "Yeah, and in the meantime your project has displaced a family of cryptids who are now wrecking your shit and posing a danger to people in the area. You've chased them until they ran into a natural boundary—this river. Maybe the kittens aren't big enough to get across it yet, or maybe Mama just decided to make a stand at the water. But whatever made her stop, she ain't running no more."

"Yeah," Geri said, her voice dark. She *really* didn't like bear traps, and I could tell she sided with the monsters a little on this one. Hell, I did too, and I figured Matt and Amy probably felt the same way. "Y'all done messed with Mother Nature, and Mama Wampus is gonna kick your ass for you."

"Fortunately for you, Tony," I said, clapping the small man hard enough on the shoulder to nearly buckle his knees. "We're from the government, and we're here to help."

13

Tony wasn't going anywhere near the woods with us, and I couldn't really blame him. If Geri was looking at me like that, I wouldn't want to intentionally go somewhere with a lot of places to hide a body, either. So me and the rest of Team Bubba (I kinda like the sound of that. Maybe I'll get t-shirts made.) walked across the muddy job site and headed into the woods.

The trail was narrow and hard to see, but we managed okay for the first few hundred yards, heading almost directly due east. But after we crossed a little stream, I couldn't find anything that looked like a path. Father Matt kinda slid past me and knelt down on the ground, looking at a branch or something.

"You gonna tell me you're a priest *and* a tracker, Padre?" I asked, half-joking.

He wasn't joking when he looked up at me and said, "Actually, yeah, I am. I was an Eagle Scout before I went to seminary and have spent a lot of time teaching wilderness survival classes at summer camps since I got my collar. The creature that made these tracks definitely has paws like a big cat, but they're slightly different from most American large felines. The prints are symmetrical, with the toes fanning out evenly from the center of the paw, not like bobcat or cougar prints. And there's an extra toe."

"Like Hemingway's cats?" Amy asked. I raised an eyebrow at her, and she shrugged. "Ernest Hemingway's cats had six toes, and it's a mutation that has passed down to their descendants. I spent some time in the Key West Field Office, and there wasn't much to do except read about the touristy stuff."

"Yes," Father Matt replied. "Like Hemingway's cats, if they were huge. Judging by the width and depth of these tracks, I'd estimate the wampus cat to be somewhere around three to four hundred pounds, and at least four feet high at the shoulder, judging by the height of broken branches I'm seeing."

"Three *hundred* pounds?" Skeeter's voice was shrill in my ear, and I winced. "Bubba, that's twice the size of most mountain lions, and a good foot or two taller! I thought these things were supposed to be the size of a bobcat."

"Yeah, bud," I replied. "I think we're hunting the Big Show of bobcats here."

"What's a big show?" Father Matt asked.

"Oh god, we're never leaving these woods," Geri muttered.

I gave my new Church liaison a pitying glance. "The Big Show is only the greatest big man in pro wrestling since Andre the Giant. He's seven and a half feet of big, bald badass, and he's a Southern boy to boot. He makes me look tiny, and that ain't the kinda thing I get to say very often. So if this wampus cat is way outside the normal size for a big cat in this part of the world, then we oughta call it Paul when we find it."

"Paul?" Father Matt was obviously woefully out of touch

in his pro wrestling viewing, and I made a vow to myself to get him to watch a whole lot of "big meaty men slapping meat." If this skinny little preacher was gonna be part of the team, he was gonna have to develop an appreciation for huge men in tiny spandex.

"Paul Wight is The Big Show's real name. It'd be kind of an in joke, us calling the big-ass cat by the real name of the World's Largest Athlete."

"Why would we call it anything?" Matt asked. "Aren't we just going to rehome it or kill it?"

Geri drew in a breath, and I knew she was about to go off on the padre, but I held up a hand. "We're gonna do everything we can *not* to kill the wampus cat. It ain't the cat's fault people are screwing with its habitat. Paul's just trying to do what animals do—hunt, eat, screw, and roll around in a sunbeam. As long as we can come up with some kind of non-lethal way to relocate the cat, we're going to."

Father Matt looked perplexed. "I was warned that you were a bloodthirsty, possibly psychotic, half-monster that needed a firm hand holding your leash. But you seem like anything but that. How did the Vatican get it so wrong about you?"

"They're not all that wrong," Geri said. "Bubba is at least half psycho most days."

"But he already has a firm hand on his leash," Amy added. "Mine." She reached out and put a hand on my forearm. "Right, honey?"

I just nodded and said, "Yes, dear."

"Plus it ain't like the Church has the best track record on who they trust," Skeeter added.

I shook my head at my best friend's version of a defense for me. "Truth be told, Matt, the Church's assessment ain't far off some days. If anybody hurts my people, they get to see how bloodthirsty I can be. I will bring down my own version of a righteous smiting on somebody's ass if they harm so much as a hair on any of these people's heads. But I try to save my real ass-kicking for them critters with coherent thought and intention. This wampus is just operating on instinct, doing what its nature demands. I can't want to kill something for doing what God intended it to do, can I?"

Father Matt shook his head, a rueful smile spreading across his narrow features. "No, you can't. And I should know better than to judge a book by its cover."

"I don't know about that," Skeeter said. "There's plenty of books where the cover sucks, and you know good and damn well that's because the book sucks."

"It's a metaphor, Skeet," I said. I might have given myself a couple of mental pats on the back for remembering the different between "metaphor" and "simile."

Skeeter's only response was a heavy sigh, then he said, "The biggest problem with having a dumbass for a best friend is that your sarcasm gets lost."

"Or does it?" I asked, feeling one corner of my mouth twitch up into a smirk. There was a tiny *beep* in my ear as Skeeter snapped off his mic in frustration. I licked my finger and made a little invisible mark in the air. One for me. I don't get too many of those, so I revel in them when I do. "Alright, Padre. Where do the tracks go from here?"

Matt pointed in a direction that was a good forty degrees off from where I thought we oughta go, so I reckon it was a good thing I wasn't leading this parade no more. I let the priest take the lead, and we slipped back into the underbrush, heading more southeast this time.

It only took us a few minutes to get to a large clearing with a ten-foot circle of disturbed dirt, scattered rocks, and lengths of heavy chain fastened to chunks of rebar sticking up out of the ground. I walked over to the nearest one and saw the chain, which looked like a logging chain with links bigger around than a bratwurst, had been snapped in two. I picked up the end and looked closer, finding telltale signs of dried blood on some of the links. "I think we found where the foreman set out his traps. There's blood on this chain."

Matt walked over, looked at the snapped chain, and went a little pale. Paler, really, since this looked like the most time he'd spent in the sun in a decade. Poor little guy had led a cloistered, sheltered life. We were throwing that right in the dumpster and lighting the whole thing on fire. "That's… incredible. Whatever was captured here snapped this chain like it was…"

"Dry spaghetti?" Geri supplied.

"A twig?" Amy suggested.

"Your leg if it gets hold of you." Everybody looked at me, but I just shrugged. "Let's put things in a framework we can all understand. This thing's sex organs are obviously in its mouth."

A trio of perplexed looks came back at me, and I barely held my giggles in as twelve-year-old me finished the joke. "Because if it gets its teeth on you, you're screwed."

A withering glare from Amy was cut short by a rustling in the trees just outside the edge of the clearing. I slapped my hand to the butt of my pistol as we all turned to see…nothing. There was nothing there. At least, not at first. We all stared off in a roughly easterly direction for a long moment, almost holding our breath waiting to get set upon by a ravening wampus, but after about thirty seconds of highest alert, I let out my breath in a long sigh.

"Well, that was a whole lot of nothing," I said, letting my hand drop from my gun.

"Umm…not exactly," Geri said, pointing. I adjusted my gaze to follow her arm, and looked a lot lower than I'd been focusing. A tiny little gray ball of fluff took a tentative step over a fallen branch, then tumbled ass over teakettle into the clearing, letting out a soft *mew* as it came to a stop, shaking dirt and leaves off its head.

"Oh my god that's thecutestthingI'veeverseeeeeeeen!" Geri's voice went hypersonic at the end as she squeed over the little furball that had somersaulted into view. I thought she was going to start hyperventilating, then the stakes got even higher as three more little fluffballs came into view.

"Oh, son of a *bitch*," I said in a low voice. "We are so screwed."

"Oh my god, they're the cutest thing *ever*!" Geri took four quick steps forward and dropped to her knees right in front of the first kitten, scooping it up and hauling it to her chest, nuzzling the baby wampus cat with her cheek and cooing at it. Cooing. The tough-as-nails monster hunter who legit tried to hunt me down and murder my ass for being part fairy (and for getting her sister killed, which was a much more reasonable motive for murder than my mom being a fairy) was now on her knees in a forest where we were pretty sure there was a giant cat that would eat our kidneys as appetizers, and she was *cuddling baby wampus cats.*

I couldn't really blame her, though. The little fur balls were adorable. They were larger than normal kittens, but not by a ton. They stood maybe six inches off the ground at the shoulder, with short, mottled coats that seemed to shift in color depending on what they were near. Some sort of natural camouflage, apparently. They were base gray, with darker and lighter spots like a sun-dappled stone floor, and they all had little balls on the end of their tails, which the lead kitten was using to thump Geri on her shoulder, eliciting giggles.

Giggles. I didn't know Geri *could* giggle. I'd been in combat with this woman, shared a house with her for the better part of a year, had seen her in the morning before coffee, watched the sun set on my back deck with her—

everything. But I had never, *ever* thought I'd ever hear her giggle. And yet here we were, with her scooping up kittens in her arms, burying her face in their fur, and giggling like a kindergartener. It was frickin' adorable.

Until the fat redneck with the hunting rifle stepped out of the woods and pointed it at me. "I'm gonna need you to tell your daughter to step away from the monsters before somebody gets hurt."

Daughter?!? Oh, somebody was getting their ass beat for that one.

14

M y *what* now?" I asked.

"His *WHAT*?!?" Geri asked, her tone possibly even more affronted than mine, which I thought was a little unnecessary. I agree that I'm not really "dad" material, except for the belly, but she didn't need to sound quite so unbelieving.

"Whatever," Dipshit the Gun-Toting Dingelberry-apotamous replied, jerking the barrel of his rifle in Geri's direction. "Daughter, niece, girlfriend, whatever. Put the creatures down and get over there with your sugar daddy." As he waved the gun in our direction, a handful of other guys, all in jeans, work boots, and orange vests that marked them as part of the construction crew, came out of the woods, all toting rifles or shotguns. That's one downside of living in the South —*everybody* owns guns, no matter their job or politics. So you just gotta assume that anybody you piss off has a 50/50 chance of going out to their truck, grabbing something persuasive off the gun rack, and coming back to continue your argument with additional persuasion.

Oh, there was no question I was going to wrap the barrel

of that .308 around his goddamned neck. Geri put the kits down and stepped over to stand next to me. Amy and Father Matt made a line on my other side, with Amy looking up at me, questions written all over her face. Questions like "are you going to do something stupid?" Or "is this going to get really, really messy?" Or even "am I going to have to cover up multiple felonies this afternoon?"

The answer to all of those would have been a resounding "yes" had a deep growl not emanated from the edge of the woods right about the time I decided that I could snatch the rifle away from the lead dumbass before he could shoot me or any of my people too much. Dipshit turned to look, and the trio of morons he was rolling with followed suit, so Geri and I just nodded at each other, took three steps forward, and decked the nearest pair of dumbasses.

Dipshit was a little out of reach, so I focused my first punch on the guy I assumed was Dipshit's kid brother, because they looked a lot alike, but relatively close in age. I mean, we were out in the woods, so it could have been a brother, a cousin, a nephew, or some very hillbilly combination of the three. Either way, he quickly shifted from "problem" to "unconscious" as my fist slammed into the hinge of his jaw and he kissed the dirt. His shotgun hit the ground but fortunately didn't go off. Especially since it was kinda pointed at my junk when it landed. That would have been awkward.

Geri was just as direct, if a little more *Road House* in her approach. She kicked one toothless methhead right in the side of his knee, and he went down just like Sam Elliott told us he would. Then she planted a knee in his nose and left him rolling around spewing blood all over the dirt. Amy was half a second behind us, but more official, yanking out her badge and yelling for Dipshit and his minions to drop their weapons.

Spoiler alert: they didn't drop their weapons. They did focus their attention on Amy, though, which allowed Father Matt to bend down, scoop up the discarded twelve-gauge, and point it at the remaining rednecks. "You should really listen to the lady," he said in a voice colder than the Bud Light waiting for me in the mini fridge on my back deck.

Dipshit didn't drop his rifle, but he stood there kinda wavering, looking back and forth between Amy with her badge and service pistol pointed at his skull, and me, with his buddy's blood on my knuckles and a big grin on my face. He had a decision to make—drop his weapon and look like a pansy in front of his friends, most of whom were too jacked up to notice that he was surrendering, or get his own ass beat and maybe shot by resisting.

He chose poorly. Dipshit focused his attention on Amy, and as he brought the barrel of his rifle up, I reached down with my right hand, grabbed Geri by the back of her belt, and flung her at him.

Yeah, I used my sidekick as a missile weapon. It happens. Not often, and not with most normal humans, but I'm a long way from normal and only part human, as the federal government has been quick to remind me. So I channeled my rage into strength, something Amy and I have been working on in training, and focused all my latent fairy power into chucking a human being at another human being. It worked. Geri flew across the twenty feet separating us from Dipshit, crashed into him, and took him down before he got a shot off.

But I might shoulda warned her that flinging an option, because as soon as she left her feet, a nonstop string of profanity flew from her lips that didn't stop until she disentangled herself from the prone Dipshit, dusted herself off, and stomped back over to where I stood grinning at her.

"You son of a *bitch*," she said, kicking me square in my left shin. "That was *not* funny!"

"Tell that to them," I said, pointing at the kittens who were no longer huddled up in a terrified ball of fluff, but were now tumbling over one another playing some weird King of Cat Mountain game that only they knew the rules to.

"Awwwww," she said, her anger melting away in the face of all that cuteness. But her adoration was quickly replaced by worry as another low growl split the clearing. "Bubba, I think Mama might be home."

"Yeah, and she might not approve of this play date," I said, staring into the woods trying to get a peek at the wampus cat. I thought I saw something moving in the underbrush, but I couldn't be sure, and if Mama shared the kittens' coloring and adaptive camouflage, I wouldn't get a good look at her until it was too damn late.

"Too damn late" came about three seconds after the thought crossed my mind, as a mottled gray-and-brown cat the size of a small panther slipped out into the clearing, barely even disturbing a branch. Mama Wampus was a magnificent creature, all sinewy muscle and glass-smooth movements. Her gaze swept the assembled humans, then locked onto her babies. She let out another little growl, and before I even saw her move, she was standing over her tumbling balls of fluff, glaring around at the humans as if daring us to touch her. I did not take up the challenge.

"Good kitty," Geri said, moving forward slowly with one hand extended. She was careful not to meet the wampus's eyes, worried it might take that as a challenge. Mama Wampus didn't pounce on her and rip her limb from limb, so I thought that was probably a good sign.

Geri eased her way across the clearing until she was almost close enough to touch the wampus, then knelt down with her hand out, palm down. Mama Wampus sniffed her hand once, twice, then kinda butted her palm with her head, and Geri responded by scratching the massive kitty behind the ears.

And that's when a giant cryptid that could have turned her entrails into outrails with one swipe of its massive claws, dropped on her belly in the dirt and started to roll around with my junior sidekick, filling the clearing with loud purrs.

"I think they like each other," Amy whispered.

"I didn't know Geri could smile that big," I replied. "Or at all."

Geri, for her part, didn't stop petting the big kitty, just reached back with her other hand and flipped me off. "I think she's calm enough not to murder anyone at the moment. Maybe you should take this chance to hogtie those assholes and relieve them of their weapons."

Seemed like a good idea to me, so Father Matt and I zip-tied the construction idiots' hands behind their backs, emptied their guns, and flung them deep into the woods. It was technically littering, but I really didn't feel like toting any extra firepower. The hand cannon dangling under my left arm was enough extra weight. I endured several minutes of lurid description about exactly what they were planning to do to me when they got loose before I smacked Dipshit upside the back of his head. That shut him up for a few seconds, but as soon as he opened his mouth again, I yanked him to his feet and spun him around so he looked right at me.

I held up another big zip tie right in front of his eyes. "You see this, asshole?"

"Yeah, I see it. You already got me tied up. What you gonna do with that?"

"Well, there's a lot of really nasty stuff I *could* do with it, but I don't wanna touch your balls. So if you don't shut the hell up right now, I'm gonna cut a hole in your top and bottom lips with my pocket knife here—" I drew one of the silver-edged kukris from my belt and held it up next to the zip tie. "And I'm gonna zip tie your goddamn mouth shut. How fun does that sound?"

He opened his mouth to reply, but I just waggled the knife and plastic tie in front of his eyes. He closed his mouth with a "snap."

"Good call," I said, patting him on the cheek. Maybe a little harder than necessary, but not harder than I *thought* was necessary.

I turned my attention back to Geri and Mama Wampus, who were now literally rolling around on the ground play-fighting like kittens. It was a little disconcerting, seeing something so lethal playing like a little kid. A little weird seeing the wampus cat do it, too. "What's the plan? We've got these assholes sorted out, but we still ain't got a solution to the real problem—development."

"He's right," Amy said, and I made a mental note of the date and time, since those words didn't get uttered often. "As long as Mama and her kits are in the path of the development, we're going to have more run-ins between wampus and humans. And those run-ins are going to get more and more dangerous until someone gets badly hurt or killed."

"Or Mama Wampus gets killed and her babies are sold off to some shitty zoo like that douche in Florida had with the were-gators," I added.

Father Matt cleared his throat. "There is someone the Church has a tenuous connection with, out in the Midwest. He runs a nature preserve for cryptids, after a fashion."

"Oh yeah," I said. "I met that guy. He's a friend of Mason's, right?"

"Yes," Father Matt replied.

"What's the Church's connection with him?" It's not that I

distrust everyone associated with organized religion, just almost everyone.

"He sometimes provides a safe refuge for cryptids that must be rehomed because one of our Hunters has found them too close to humans. There's no official relationship, but sometimes we will do favors for each other. I feel like housing a mother wampus cat and her litter would be right up his alley."

"Sounds good," Amy said. "Can you call him? I can get everything arranged for transport, but before we go trying to tranq Mama and get her into a cage, I'd like to know we definitely have a place for her to go."

"Yes, I can make a call," Matt said, stepping off into the edge of the woods and pulling out a satellite phone I didn't know he'd been carrying. I might have to start paying attention to this dude if he kept on being useful. Especially if the check cleared *and* he wasn't completely dead weight in the field.

Matt punched in a few numbers, then froze as I heard a branch snap off in the woods just outside the clearing. I whirled around, looking in the direction of the sound, but Mama Wampus was way faster than me. She was on her feet and putting herself in between the sound and her babies before I'd even locked in on where the noise came from. That low growl was back, but this time her ears were flat, her tail was extended low behind her, and I could see the corners of her mouth creeping up in a snarl. She made a low sound, and her kits all huddled up together behind Geri, peeking around her legs as she got to her feet with her pistol drawn.

Mama Wampus let out another growl that grew until it was a kind of yowl that sounded like a cross between a cougar and a freight train, and took a couple of steps toward the edge of the woods. Another rustling crack came from off to our right, and we all turned to look that way, Mama included. This time she let out a serious *roar*, a full-throated cry of challenge and rage that someone interrupted her play-time and may have threatened her babies. Mama was *pissed*.

She spun her head back around to face the original source of the sound and bunched up her legs as if ready to pounce. There was another, much louder, *crack*, this one followed by two more, and red blossomed on Mama Wampus's sides as three large-caliber bullets ripped into her. She whirled around, crying out in shock and pain, looking for what hurt her, and I watched in horror as her back legs gave out, then her front, and she collapsed to the dirt.

Geri rushed over to her and dropped to her knees, trying frantically to put pressure on the wounds, but the big cat was already gone. She was dead before her head hit the ground. Geri sprang to her feet and turned in a circle, rage mottling her face. "Who's out there? Show yourself, you son of a bitch!"

"Okay," came a voice from the woods. "But we've got all of you covered, so please don't do anything stupid. I'm mostly talking to you, Brabham. Your reputation precedes you."

EPILOGUE

The voice belonged to a muscular man carrying a military-looking rifle with a grenade launcher slung under the barrel. He was a little over six feet tall, with dark skin and a neat goatee. His brown eyes were cold as ice chips, and the look on his face was not that of a man one should screw with. He wore black tactical gear, and there was a Velcro label on the front of his flak jacket that read "PEST CONTROL."

Two others in similar garb stepped out of the woods on either side of us, covering us with guns of their own. They all wore "Pest Control" on their vests, and they all looked way too comfortable with the idea of shooting us all.

"What the fuck was that? Who the fuck are you? What are you doing out here?" Geri shouted, tears streaming down her face. Her hand twitched, and I could see the effort she was putting into not drawing down on the man who had an assault rifle pointed right at her chest.

"Same as you, cookie," the man said. "My job. Only difference is, I'm good at mine. Now all y'all drop your gear and go sit in the dirt where you can't bother anybody. Get in the way, and I'll put a bullet in your face. There's plenty of space here for me to dig graves."

For once, we did as we were told. I sat down at the base of a tree and watched as the Lead Asshole waved his Hench-Assholes over. One was a white woman, stocky and muscular, with short blond hair and an acne-speckled jawline that screamed steroid abuse. The other was a thick-necked Asian man who looked like a powerlifter or college wrestler, and he carried a massive machine gun instead of an AR-15 or whatever the other two dickheads were toting. It wasn't the ridiculous minigun the genetically altered half-cryptid freaks I'd run into with Harker carried, but it was about as big a damn weapon as I could imagine a human being carrying. This dude was *stout*.

We sat there for a couple minutes before the roar of engines came to us through the trees. A quartet of ATVs crashed through the brush, breaking their own trail where none existed, and pulled to a stop. My blood started to boil even more when I saw the collapsible cage on a small trailer behind one of the four-wheelers. They weren't just murdering assholes. They were murdering, *kidnapping* assholes. I swore to Mama Wampus's spirit that I'd get justice for her, no matter what it took. I felt a little tingle run through me, and it felt like my fairy magic considered that kind of promise very serious. That was fine by me, I was pretty serious, too. Seriously *pissed*.

We sat in the dirt as the Pest Control pricks loaded all the kits into the cage, and all our weapons into a duffel one of the Hench-Assholes opened up.

"I'll be coming for that stuff," I said.

The Asian man grinned down at me and patted the barrel of his machine gun. "Come on, redneck. I'll be waiting."

I'm used to being the guy with the biggest gun in the

room, and I don't like it when somebody threatens me, so I smiled back at Asian Hench-Asshole and said, "Good."

He looked a little disturbed at me not being afraid of him, like that didn't happen much with this bunch, and took a couple steps back toward where his pals were loading the four-wheelers. A couple minutes later, and they were gone, along with all our weapons except for pocketknives. I mean, I assumed everybody else carried a pocketknife. Everybody but Amy, because she was raised civilized.

We got up and all just kinda stood there for a moment, the rest of my team as surprised as me, then I walked over to the dead wampus cat. I knelt by her body and patted her head. "I'm sorry, Mama Kitty. But I promise you this, we will save those babies." Then I stood up and turned to my team— Amy, furiously tapping on her sat phone looking for answers, Matt, swiping his finger across the screen of his phone trying to get a signal, and Geri just standing there, fury and sorrow radiating off her in waves as she stood with tears streaming down her face.

"I've just got two questions," I said. Everyone turned to me, and I continued. "Who the fuck is Pest Control, and where do we go to kick their ass?"

THIRTY-PLUS THOUSAND FEET OVERHEAD, a monitor flickered to life. A shadowy figure appeared on the screen, bathing the cabin of the Gulfstream in bluish light. "I trust everything went according to plan?" the figure asked.

"Yes, Director," said one of the men sitting in plush leather seats. He held a flute of champagne in one hand and an unlit cigar in the other. A proud smile split his square face, and he said, "The redneck and his people didn't know what hit them."

"Do not underestimate Brabham and his associates. They have surprised us in the past," the figure said.

"Don't sweat it, Boss," said an Asian man with bulging biceps from another chair. "If he comes for us, we'll take him out. No big deal."

"Others have tried, and failed," the figure said. "Do not provoke them directly, or I will not be there to bail you out when it goes poorly."

"I'm not worried about that moron," the Asian man replied with a snort.

"But we do have a healthy respect for the abilities of his associates," said the first man. "His tech officer is first rate, Deputy Director Hall is a formidable adversary in the field and in the office, and the woman Geri is…unpredictable."

"And that makes her dangerous, we know." This comment came from a stocky woman sitting near the back of the plane. "Come on, we got the kitties, killed the mother, sent a message to Bubba and his cronies, and got away without a scratch. Let us have the win, Boss."

The figure's shoulders bobbed up and down as if in unheard laughter. "Of course, Karen. Celebrate your victory. Enjoy the mini bar, and there will be a car at the airport to take you to a fine victory dinner when you return to base."

Smiles and high-fives circled the cabin. When the boss bought dinner, it was usually at a place that made Morton's look like McDonald's, and nothing was off limits, even the stuff on the tippy-top shelf. "But Chad?" The figure spoke again, and the crew fell silent.

"Yes, Boss?" the first man replied.

"Be in the office at eight tomorrow morning or I'll cut off one toe for every member of your team that's late." Then the figure leaned forward to press the "OFF" button on their computer, and as they did, a curl of blond hair peeked out from under the hood they wore to obscure their features.

The team exchanged worried glances. This was the first identifying feature the Boss had allowed any of them to see in the nine months since Pest Control had been founded to eradicate all cryptids and protect humanity from the growing threat of human-cryptid breeding. The Boss had been incredibly private up to this point, and the last thing they wanted was to be on their…*her* bad side.

As the screen went black, Chad stood up and faced his team. "Nobody saw what we saw, okay? There was no lock of hair that slipped free, and nobody got a look at the back of her hand, right?"

One by one, every member of Pest Control shook their heads. No one had seen anything. Chad nodded. "Good. We all remember what happened to Chavez, right? I still don't know what he saw, but I know what he's seeing now—nothing. So we do our job, we hunt monsters, and we beat the shit out of anybody who protects them. Especially any fat, tattooed rednecks from Georgia." Chad reached down and patted the orange "T" on his forearm. "But when we finally get the green light to take his mongrel ass down, Bubba Brabham is *mine*. He might not have recognized me back there in the woods, but I remember him. Me and Bubba have got some catching up to do, and this time I plan on him being the one leaving in an ambulance."

He finished off his champagne, then looked around at his team. "Or maybe he leaves in a hearse."

TO BE CONTINUED

ABOUT THE AUTHOR

John G. Hartness is a teller of tales, a righter of wrong, defender of ladies' virtues, and some people call him Maurice, for he speaks of the pompatus of love. He is also the best-selling author of EPIC-Award-winning series *The Black Knight Chronicles* from Bell Bridge Books, a comedic urban fantasy series that answers the eternal question "Why aren't there more fat vampires?" In July of 2016. John was honored with the Manly Wade Wellman Award by the NC Speculative Fiction Foundation for Best Novel by a North Carolina writer in 2015 for the first Quincy Harker novella, *Raising Hell.*

In 2016, John teamed up with a pair of other publishing industry ne'er-do-wells and founded Falstaff Books, a publishing company dedicated to pushing the boundaries of literature and entertainment.

In his copious free time John enjoys long walks on the beach, rescuing kittens from trees and getting caught in the rain. An avid *Magic: the Gathering* player, John is strong in his nerd-fu and has sometimes been referred to as "the Kevin Smith of Charlotte, NC." And not just for his girth.

Find out more about John online
www.johnhartness.com

STAY IN TOUCH!

If you enjoyed this book, please leave a review on Amazon, Goodreads, or wherever you like.

If you'd like to hear more about or from the author, please join my mailing list at https://www.subscribepage.com/g8d0a9.

You can get some free short stories just for signing up, and whenever a book gets 50 reviews, the author gets a unicorn. I need another unicorn. The ones I have are getting lonely. So please leave a review and get me another unicorn!

Comes a Reckoning

Histories: A Quincy Harker, Demon Hunter Collection

Histories II: A Quincy Harker, Demon Hunter Collection

SHINGLES

Zombies Ate My Homework: Shingles Book 5

Slow Ride: Shingles Book 12

Carnival of Psychos: Shingles Book 19

Jingle My Balls: Shingles Book 24

Snatched: Grandma Annie and the Cooter of Doom: Shingles Book 29

Deader than Hell: Shingles Book 40

OTHER WORK

The True Confessions of Fandingo the Fantastical (with EM Kaplan)

Queen of Kats

Fireheart

Amazing Grace: A Dead Old Ladies Detective Agency Mystery

From the Stone

The Chosen

Genesis

Hazard Pay and Other Tales

Have Spacecat, Will Travel

Identity Theft

FRIENDS OF FALSTAFF

Printed in Great Britain
by Amazon

31383148R00071